Love Song

Also From Kylie Scott

The Rich Boy

Lies

Repeat

It Seemed Like a Good Idea at the Time

Trust

THE DIVE BAR SERIES
Dirty
Twist
Chaser

THE STAGE DIVE SERIES
Lick
Play
Lead
Deep
Strong: A Stage Dive Novella

THE FLESH SERIES
Flesh
Skin
Flesh Series Novellas

Heart's a Mess

Colonist's Wife

Love Song

A Stage Dive Novella

By Kylie Scott

1001 DARK NIGHTS

PRESS

Love Song
A Stage Dive Novella
By Kylie Scott

Copyright 2020 Kylie Scott
ISBN: 978-1-951812-17-1

Cover photo credit © Annie Ray/ Passion Pages

Published by 1001 Dark Nights Press, an imprint of Evil Eye
Concepts, Incorporated

Sign up for the 1001 Dark Nights Newsletter
and be entered to win a Tiffany Key necklace.

There's a contest every month!

Go to www.1001DarkNights.com to subscribe.

**As a bonus, all subscribers can download
FIVE FREE exclusive books!**

One Thousand and One Dark Nights

Once upon a time, in the future…

*I was a student fascinated with stories and learning.
I studied philosophy, poetry, history, the occult, and
the art and science of love and magic. I had a vast
library at my father's home and collected thousands
of volumes of fantastic tales.*

*I learned all about ancient races and bygone
times. About myths and legends and dreams of all
people through the millennium. And the more I read
the stronger my imagination grew until I discovered
that I was able to travel into the stories… to actually
become part of them.*

*I wish I could say that I listened to my teacher
and respected my gift, as I ought to have. If I had, I
would not be telling you this tale now.
But I was foolhardy and confused, showing off
with bravery.*

*One afternoon, curious about the myth of the
Arabian Nights, I traveled back to ancient Persia to
see for myself if it was true that every day Shahryar
(Persian: شهريار, "king") married a new virgin, and then
sent yesterday's wife to be beheaded. It was written
and I had read, that by the time he met Scheherazade,
the vizier's daughter, he'd killed one thousand
women.*

*Something went wrong with my efforts. I arrived
in the midst of the story and somehow exchanged
places with Scheherazade – a phenomena that had
never occurred before and that still to this day, I
cannot explain.*

*Now I am trapped in that ancient past. I have
taken on Scheherazade's life and the only way I can
protect myself and stay alive is to do what she did to
protect herself and stay alive.*

*Every night the King calls for me and listens as I spin tales.
And when the evening ends and dawn breaks, I stop at a
point that leaves him breathless and yearning for more.
And so the King spares my life for one more day, so that
he might hear the rest of my dark tale.*

*As soon as I finish a story... I begin a new
one... like the one that you, dear reader, have before
you now.*

Playlist

"Somebody That I Used To Know" by Gotye
"Moanin' At Midnight" by Howlin' Wolf
"Let It Go" by James Bay
"Ex-Factor" by Lauryn Hill
"Always On My Mind" by Willie Nelson
"Exile" by Taylor Swift feat Bon Iver
"Go Your Own Way" by Fleetwood Mac
"Try" by P!nk
"Chew on My Heart" by James Bay

Chapter One

"No," said the bodyguard.

"But—"

"Miss, do you have any idea how many people try to get backstage by claiming they have some sort of relationship with Mr. Dillon?" Face a careful blank, the man in the slick black suit stared down at me. He had a point. I'd pushed through a crush of fans, getting my toes stomped on several times, along with taking an elbow to the kidney, just to talk to this guy. God only knew what it took to get near the star of the show.

"I'd imagine a lot," I yelled back at him. Necessary given the volume of the music filling the space. "The difference here is I'm not lying."

"But since everyone says that, you can see from my perspective how that's not actually a point of difference."

Adam Dillon, rock star extraordinaire, gyrated his slim denim-clad hips like an Alt-Rock Elvis on the nearby stage. He pouted and crooned about the woman who'd done him wrong. Me. That's right, I was the big bad ex who'd broken him and woke him to the dangers of love. Or so the song said.

The song lied and then some.

According to the lyrics he was currently wailing, I'd ground his heart beneath my five-inch heels before blowing him a kiss goodbye.

From memory, there'd been a lot of shouting, but no blowing of kisses. And having just kicked off the flats I wore for work, I'd been barefoot, my legs and back aching. No way had I been strutting around in stilettos. Home from a hard day at the hair salon, I'd returned to find Adam on the couch. The same place he'd been when I'd left for work approximately eleven hours earlier. The same place he'd been for what felt like months as I worked my ass off to pay the rent. That's when all hell broke loose. However, it wasn't the only issue that had caused our relationship to bomb. *Nothing's ever simple.*

But back to the here and now. I grabbed the slip of paper out of my front pocket, holding it up for his perusal. "My name is Jill Schwartz. How many of those people claiming to know him have one of these?"

His eyes widened as he scanned the name on the check, before widening again at the amount. And fair enough too. I'd had a mild panic attack myself when it had first arrived. When Adam decided to make a statement, he didn't bother with subtle. If only I could figure out what it all meant. If it meant anything at all, of course. And that question was what had brought me here tonight.

The bodyguard looked me over more carefully this time. His expression remained unimpressed. Understandable, given I didn't resemble a rock star's girlfriend, past or present. A bit below average height, sharp chin, pronounced cheekbones, olive skin, and a resting bitch face that was the envy of many. Or so I liked to think. I was basically a squirrel with attitude, who didn't mind cracking the odd nut or two to get things done.

Meanwhile, Adam with his long dark hair, tattoos, and lanky body had appeared perfectly at home on the cover of *Rolling Stone* magazine the month before. He'd been sitting cross-legged on a Persian rug, strumming an acoustic guitar. It wasn't hard to see how the bodyguard might struggle to imagine us as an item worthy of all this musical angst.

"Would you happen to have some ID on you, ma'am?" he asked.

I fished out my wallet from my jeans' pocket. Not easy to do with the heaving mass of sweaty bodies around me, cramming me in on every angle. I produced my license, and he shone a little flashlight on it. "It's from last year so my hair was a lot longer," I explained. "And blue."

The corner of his mouth twitched, but he gave no other reaction.

Blue hair had been great. From turquoise to indigo and back again. All of my childhood mermaid dreams come to life. Right now, however, it'd been cut to around shoulder blade-length and dyed silver and gray. Very kickass.

Next the security dude pulled out a slick little walkie-talkie and issued a series of orders. Another guy, this one in black jeans and a matching tee, joined him at the gate. Now it was his turn to look me up and down in mild disbelief. But then the gate carefully opened, and they ushered me through. A couple of the fans nearby complained bitterly and offered bribes (of both sexual and monetary nature). But no-go. Only I was permitted into the inner sanctum. Amazing. It had actually worked. I was really going to get to see him again after all this time. Every speech I'd prepared earlier disappeared from my head, and my hands started shaking for reasons I'd rather not ponder.

Up some stairs and into the elusive, exclusive backstage area the bodyguard and I went. A high wall sheltered us from the actual stage and its surrounds. But it soon opened to a larger corridor with people rushing back and forth. The banging vibration of the bass seemed to seep through the walls, the music loud enough to make my ears ring. We made a sharp right turn, and the sort of industrial look gave way to a slick little lounge with a bar and fridge, a large arrangement of white orchids, bottles of water lined up on a side table, a glass bowl full of M&Ms (Adam's favorite), and an Amazonian woman busy with her cell. Tall, brunette, vaguely terrifying, and wearing a pair of fifties-style Saint Laurent platform heels I'd had wet dreams of owning. Oh, good Lord, those shoes. I could have drooled. A cheap knockoff of them sat at home in my wardrobe. I was still saving them for a special occasion. But not this sort of special occasion. Coming here tonight, doing this, had seemed like more of a combat boot kind of situation. Storming the rock 'n' roll castle and all that.

"Thanks, Ziggy," she said, dismissing the bodyguard before her gaze flicked over me with obvious disinterest. "You've got sixty seconds. Talk."

"And who the hell might you be?" I asked, not so politely, refusing to be cowed.

At this, she smiled. "I'm Martha, Adam's manager, and you?"

"Jill. Adam's ex. But I'm sure the bodyguard already told you that."

The speculative look in her eyes increased some hundred-fold. "So, what do you want, Adam's ex?"

"To talk to Adam about something he sent me recently."

She raised her chin. "The check. I didn't know he'd done that."

"You know everything he does?"

"Basically," she said, tone blasé. "You have to understand, rock stars are all big, whiny babies who need someone running their lives, or everything goes to hell in a handbasket. For Adam, I am that someone. Next question. If the check is real, and you are who you say you are, why not just take the money and run?"

I sighed. "I thought about it. That album has been the bane of my existence ever since it came out. I can't go anywhere without hearing the damn thing. Bars, gas stations, the grocery store…it's like I'm being musically stalked."

"The songs aren't exactly complimentary toward you," she allowed.

At this, I rolled my eyes. A terrible habit, but I couldn't help myself. If someone said something breathtakingly obvious, my first impulse was always the silent and deadly, *duh*. "I'm not getting into that with you. It's private. Well, it should be private. Though it would be fair to say that Adam's version of our relationship and mine differ significantly. But the fact is, he's been working on making it in the music business since long before I met him. It was his dream, and he worked hard and saw it through. Kudos to him. If he'd just sent me his share of the rent and so on for the period we lived together, then I wouldn't be here right now. Because this check…it's too much. Way too much."

"Seven digits is impressive. But he can afford it, if that's your concern."

"I'm sure he can, but that's not the point."

"You've never given any interviews about him. Never sold any photos from when you were together. I'd have been alerted to it if you had."

"And?"

Her gaze scanned my body, up and down. "Are you pregnant?"

"No."

"Do you hope to get pregnant?"

"Good Lord. Get your mind out of my uterus. I just want to talk to him about the check."

For a long moment, the manager chick, Martha, just stared at me. Then she said, "Interesting. Come with me."

Then she was off, striding in those elegant towering high heels. I bet she could sprint in those suckers. It was like the whole world was her runway and she had places to be.

"Where are we going?" I asked, not quite jogging to keep up. Short legs sucked sometimes.

"You want to talk to Adam?"

"Well, yes, but…"

"Yes or no, Jill? I don't have time to screw around."

"Yes, I want to talk to him," I said, brows drawn down. "I need to talk to him."

The various dressing rooms and storerooms and who knew what else gave way to larger hallways. Props, lights, and all sorts of things sat in neat piles here and there. Plenty of people moved to and fro, and more just hung around. Out through a pair of big double doors, and we were in a tunnel with a couple of security guards waiting alongside a large, shiny black Mercedes Benz SUV.

Martha opened the car's back door. Once more, her cell sat in her hand, her gaze glued to the screen. "Get in."

I hesitated. Of course, I did. Because where I came from, being lured into vehicles by relative strangers was generally believed to be a bad thing. And this woman didn't even have the decency to first offer me candy or a kitten.

"I repeat, I do not have time to screw around. In a little less than two minutes' time, Adam will be rushed straight through the backstage area and out here to the car," said Martha, sounding vaguely bored. "Your choices are either getting in said vehicle, or having Bon return you to the audience area. Which will it be?"

The security dude gave me a glance. Pretty sure those bulges beneath his suit coat weren't from carrying an excess of chewing gum or Kleenex. Nope. Bon was packing. How insane this whole world was.

"Truth is, I shouldn't even be doing this," she continued. "But you've ever so slightly woken my cold dead heart. Turns out, I happen to know what it's like to be in your position. Someone wrote an album about me once, too. Not what you'd call a pleasant experience."

Huh. Though, in Martha's case, I'd hazard a guess that any lyrics about grinding a guy's heart beneath five-inch heels would be deadly accurate.

She tapped her foot against the concrete. "So?"

"Where will Adam be going?" I asked, stalling.

"Straight home, if I have anything to say about it. But I can't guarantee that." Her eyebrows bent with the merest hint of a frown. "Sometimes he can struggle to unwind after a show."

Interesting. I resisted the urge to smile at the irony. I'd had trouble getting Adam off the couch. And now it seemed the new woman in his life had trouble keeping him there.

In all honesty, the whole situation was kind of doing my head in. Adam's new life could officially be labeled: *crazy town*. Bodyguards and luxury cars and this terrifying woman running everything. Back when I knew him, all of a year ago, he'd owned exactly one pair of socks, and they both had holes in them. Not so sexy. You can guess what he got for Christmas that year. He spent his days writing songs or jamming with friends at various bars around town. Sometimes, he'd manage to get paid for a gig or land some delivery work at a pizza place. Do a few shifts behind the bar at a local club. But that was about as far as his behaving like a responsible adult went. He'd couch surfed for years, living with various friends and acquaintances, until he and I hooked up. Now this was his life.

Mind blown.

"You can talk to him on the drive to wherever he goes, then Mac will take you wherever you want," said Martha. "In a couple of days, Adam's on a plane to start the European leg of his tour. Trust me when I say this is the only opportunity you're going to get to talk to him face-to-face in the foreseeable future. Do you want it or not?"

Oh, man. I really shouldn't have, but I climbed into the SUV, sliding across the black leather seat to the far side. The interior was pristine with that new-car smell. In days gone by, he'd borrowed my crappy old hatchback to get places. Wedging guitar cases and amps into the small vehicle with amazing skill. Now this. How far the boy had come.

The large handsome dark-skinned man sitting in the driver's seat gave me a smile in the rearview mirror. "Miss."

"Hello." My smile wobbled, the most likely cause being my lack of confidence. Which was crazy. Adam Dillon had never intimidated me a day in his life. As beautiful and talented as he might be, it was hard to be unsettled by someone who constantly forgot to put the toilet seat down. It had to be this situation—the concert, the limousine, the security. I'd be fine in a minute. Give me a chance to catch my breath and I'd be...

And there he was, a towel perched hoodlike on his head, and a bottle of Gatorade attached to his lips. One bodyguard in front, and another bringing up the rear. Martha marched beside him, her mouth moving with what I assumed was an endless stream of information. Occasionally, Adam nodded in reply. He wore sneakers, jeans, and a tee. The shirt was bathed in sweat, clinging to his skin. Guess it got hot under those spotlights. And he had more room to strut around than on the tiny stages at the little gigs he'd done when he was with me.

But that wasn't all. While he'd looked like a quintessential rock god on the stage, as he drew nearer, I could see that his face was pale, and there were bruises beneath his eyes. To put it mildly, he looked like shit. And yet, all I could do was stare.

It was probably just the shock of seeing him again after so long. I mean, I'd seen him. Hell. I could hardly avoid him on billboards and the internet and all the rest. Sometimes with beautiful women draped over him, and sometimes without. Wasn't that just fucking delightful? But experiencing him again in the flesh seemed like something else entirely. Something I apparently hadn't been quite as prepared for as I'd hoped.

A woman dashed up behind the group, waving a piece of paper and a pen. And she was gorgeous, dammit. A statuesque redhead with ample cleavage spilling out of her barely tied-on top. She shrieked Adam's name in what I guessed to be some sort of groupie come hither mating call. Glass would have shattered at the high pitch she managed, though Adam didn't even flinch. Didn't even acknowledge her existence. The rear security dude stopped her progress, and that was that.

Where were these hordes of fans a short year ago when he was playing to half-empty clubs and selling CDs from the trunk of my car? He was the same guy playing the same music back then. Better music, actually. More honest. Less me-being-a-bitch-centric, which I was bound to appreciate.

"To the club, Mac," said Adam, climbing into the vehicle, obviously not having seen me. There he was, rock 'n' roll's newest darling and my ex-boyfriend.

Martha all but growled. "Straight home, Mac. I mean it!"

"You're not my real mother," grumbled the rock star.

"I'm not your mother at all, you idiot. Now enough with the partying. Go home and get some rest, Adam. Or else." She turned to go, then paused. "By the way, there's a problem with the parking level access gates at the apartment building so you'll need to go through the front door."

Mac just nodded.

"And there's one other potential issue on the horizon tonight," Martha continued. "But for that one, you're on your own. Enjoy."

Adam opened his mouth to say something, but then he followed her pointed gaze and spied me hiding in the corner. He stopped cold. The man totally froze. Bambi in headlights had nothing on him. His brows rose, and his eyes went as wide as the moon. "Jill?"

"Hi." My one-syllable greeting seemed a bit of an underwhelming start to our so-we-meet-again-my-nemesis moment. "Hey," I added.

Notice my amazing conversational skills at play. To think I rehearsed this meeting multiple times in the mirror.

"What the fuck?" He turned back to Martha, who helpfully shut the door in his face with a sly sort of smile. You'd almost think she was enjoying herself. Bon the bodyguard climbed into the front passenger seat, and we were moving.

"Seatbelts, please," said Mac.

Both Adam and I did as told while giving each other wary looks. Now I'd known it would be difficult to get near him. He had a posse of people around him these days for protection and other purposes. And I'd known it would be awkward as all hell to talk to him again after all this time. However, I'd had no idea it would be this bad. My heart stuttered, and my brain stalled. I'd thought I was over him. I mean, I was. I definitely completely had to be. Yet even reeking of sweat and clearly exhausted, he continued to play havoc with my hormones.

This was awful. A terrible mistake. I should have just texted him maybe. Or taken the money and never gone near him again. Much safer for my heart and soul.

"It's really you," he said, a line forming between his brows. About as much as he committed to being curious about anything outside of music. One small line. "What are you doing here?"

"You sent me that check," I said, tone terse.

"Yeah?"

"Well, it's a bit excessive, don't you think?"

He just shrugged, pushing back the towel half covering his face. "Figured you helped support me while I was coming up. Plus, you were sort of the inspiration for some of the songs, so…"

"Sort of?" I just blinked. "Which ones?"

"What?" He blinked back at me. There was always something boyish in his gaze that got to me. Something pure, almost. He loved what he loved, and as far as he was concerned, it just was that straightforward and simple. Not that any of that mattered anymore. Right now, he just seemed tired and confused.

"Which songs was I *sort of* the inspiration for?" I asked, pushing onward.

He took a long pull on the bottle of Gatorade. "You know."

"No, I don't, actually. Though I'd very much like to."

Nothing from him.

"I'm a little perplexed, Adam. You see, I thought you'd written the whole damn album about how abhorrent I was. All about what an utter backstabbing, Satan-worshipping hussy I turned out to be. I mean, you basically told the entire world I was the worst of the worst. But apparently, it was only some of the songs. What a relief. Phew." I blew out a breath. "So, which ones?"

"Jill—"

"How about *Hard Little Heart*? Did I inspire that one?"

"Um."

I tapped a finger against my lips. "'*She's solid rotten to the core, guaranteed to make your heart sore.*' Those are the lyrics, right?"

"Yeah, but—"

"And *Devil in the Woman*?"

"I kind of take inspiration from everywhere," he blurted out, sounding all sorts of soundbite and desperate. The idiot.

I cocked my head. "That's strange. I could have sworn in that interview for *Music Monthly* that you'd only ever been in one serious relationship in your life, and it was the basis for almost all of your recent music."

"You've been following me online?"

"Focus."

"Right," he said. "Well, I meant what I said. Almost all of the music."

Mac gave us an amused glance in the rearview mirror. Beside him, Bon shifted in his seat slightly, all the better to watch me out of the corner of his eye. That the bodyguard considered me a threat was kind of cool. A huge bolster to my wounded ego.

"What about *Better Off Gone*?" I asked. "I like that one. It's sort of bluesy. I mean, the woman you're singing about obviously ruined your whole existence for all of space and time, but still...nice tune."

His gaze skipped about the interior of the vehicle. "Um, yeah, I don't really remember. Look, about the money—"

"Unless of course when you were talking about the songs being written about the most important and meaningful relationship you'd ever been in, the love of your life that broke your heart into a million tiny little razor-edged pieces, you didn't in fact mean me. Was that it?"

He scowled, appearing truly put out. "You know I meant you."

"Wow. Now we're getting somewhere. Okay," I said through gritted teeth. "Is this the same relationship where you sprinkled your assorted crap throughout the entire apartment like an indie-rock trash fairy, contributed to household finances solely in the form of cold leftover pepperoni pizza, and missed my birthday dinner because someone invited you to jam at the last minute?"

"I already apologized for that. And you like pizza!"

Bon turned a chuckle into a cough in the front seat. Very professionally done.

I just groaned. "Tell me you've achieved some small modicum of personal growth involving some healthy self-realization in the last year. Please."

Streetlights and nighttime traffic flowed by outside as we made our way through Portland's downtown area. I'd heard he had an apartment nearby in the Pearl District. If you wanted hip clothes, restaurants, or just the best bookshop in the entire world, it was the place to be. Not that I could afford it, usually.

And all the while, Adam just sat there, watching me with his dark eyes. "You're still angry, huh?"

"*Still* angry? No, I was coasting along just fine with simmering resentment until your check arrived, resulting in this conversation and your half-assed denials. Now I'm furious."

"Miss Schwartz," said Bon from the front of the vehicle. "While I realize that my client has given you a certain cause for anger. I'd ask that you not assault him while we're in a moving vehicle. It's dangerous for everyone involved."

"I'm not going to hit him," I answered, outraged. "I'm a pacifist."

He just nodded toward the two clenched fists sitting in my lap.

"Oh. We're just talking. Civilly. Sort of." Slowly, I stretched out my fingers, rubbing them against the legs of my black skinny jeans. "I'm a very nice person once you get to know me."

"Of course you are, miss."

"I've never hit anyone in my life." I frowned. "Where was I?"

"Didn't we already have this fight when you threw me out?" asked Adam, shoving a frustrated hand through his long hair. Which was seriously long, by the way. Nearing Rapunzel status. It didn't look as if he'd cut it in forever.

I thought his question over, tapping a finger thoughtfully against my lips. "No. That was a different one. You've fucked up in multiple and unforeseen ways since then. It's mind-blowing, really."

He just sighed.

"You'd mentioned that Adam failed to pick up his shit, never paid for anything, and missed your birthday dinner," supplied Mac in a cheerful tone. "Not much of a surprise that you kicked him out, if you ask me. He was asking for it."

Adam slumped back in the seat with a groan. "Remind me why I pay you again, Mac?"

"You pay me to drive," answered the chauffeur. "My opinions, however, are my own and thrown in for free. You're welcome."

"Great."

"Honest to God, I gave him so many chances, Mac. You wouldn't believe it." I took a deep breath and refocused on the cause of all of my aggravation. "And here's the bit that gets me. If I really was this great love of your life, Adam, the one that rocked you to your core, worthy of writing all of these horrendous yet strangely catchy tunes about, then why did you never tell me you loved me?"

At that, he froze in terror once more. If we hadn't been speeding down a busy street, he might have made a move for the door, thrown himself out, and taken his chances with the oncoming traffic. The man looked that desperate.

"You've told every music journalist on the planet, it seems. Screamed it from the stage in every other song. Heck, the word even made the title of *Lovestricken*. But you never told me, not even once." My eyes started to itch for some weird reason. Let's not question why. "Why is that exactly?"

He pressed his lips into a tight line. "Can't you just take the check and call it an apology?"

"Why didn't you tell me you loved me?"

"We've been over for ages. Why does this even matter?"

"Well, it matters because you've been talking about me and singing about me pretty much constantly for a while now, Adam. Makes it kind of hard to put everything in the past, in all honesty."

Nothing from him.

"In fact, I think it's time I had my say," I said. "So why didn't you tell me?"

He turned his face away, the streetlights casting shadows on the sharp lines of his cheekbones and the shape of his lips. God, he was beautiful. Even in his exhausted, rundown state, I couldn't help but stare, and my heart gave the most embarrassing lurch. Life would be so much simpler if I didn't still swoon at the sight of him. At the thought of him. The more time passed, the more my head seemed to forget how aggravating he was in a thousand tiny everyday ways, but my heart still remembered perfectly what it had been like to fall for him.

"Three little words," I said. "Can't be that hard."

"I don't know," he mumbled.

"Bullshit."

"It was never the right time."

"Oh, please." My throat tightened, and my vision swam. Ugh. "You never loved me. Our relationship was convenient for you. A place to live and someone to do your laundry. I was just an easy—"

He hung his head. "Fuck's sake. You have got to be kidding me."

"What?"

"You and me, we were never convenient. And you and easy have nothing in common. Trust me on that one."

"You utter douche canoe."

"I worshipped the ground you walked on."

"You grunted at me and called it a conversation. No wonder I missed the signs of your supposed adulation." I ground my teeth together. "Just admit it already. The whole being in love with me thing is bullshit. It's a PR stunt or a...a..."

"Are you crying?"

"No!"

"Jill." He leaned closer, cupping my face in his big hand. His gaze went from curious to startled in under a second. "Jesus, you are."

I pushed off his hand. "I am not crying, I'm just very angry at you, and it's coming out in unexpected ways."

"We're here," announced the bodyguard.

Sure enough, out on the sidewalk, a group of fans waited along with several photographers waving their cameras around. I wiped the tears off my face. Stupid emotions. Righteous fury was what I was feeling. Not pain and heartache. I got over Adam a long time ago with the aid of ice-cream, vodka, and my most excellent girl gang. Those three things trumped a male of the species any day of the week. It was just that smelling him and hearing him and seeing him again had me confused or something.

In all likelihood, I was crying due to his presence giving me horrific flashbacks. To such occasions as when I went to visit my parents for a week and came back to find the interior of the fridge somehow entirely covered in black mold. Or the time I came home from work to find the furniture rearranged into the sign of the anti-Christ in honor of Ozzy Osbourne. Perhaps even the memory of when he wrote a song for me on the living room wall in permanent marker. A love song, almost, but without actually going so far as the L-word, of course. Because…Adam.

Actually, I didn't hate that particular memory. I might have even taken a photo of the wall before I invited the girls over to graffiti all over it. But I still very much hated him and should tell him as much. Right now.

"I hate you, and I'm perfectly fucking fine," I sobbed. "I am so…so over you, Adam Dillon. S-so…"

"Goddammit," he snarled, reaching for me.

Chapter Two

Everything seemed to happen at once. The bodyguard cleared a space outside and opened the car door. Adam snaked a hand around my waist and dragged me up against him and out of the vehicle. Lights flashed and people shouted. Basically, all hell broke loose. Again.

"What are you doing?" I whisper-screeched.

"I'm not leaving you like this. We're going inside." And that was that.

My feet barely touched the ground. In fact, they definitely didn't due to my wrapping them around his waist. It just seemed safer since the man had gone insane and seemed determined to carry me off so we could continue our fight elsewhere. If he was so desperate to get cried on and yelled at, then I was certainly the girl to do it. Easy, as he carted me through the waiting crowd. With one hand on my ass, he used the other to cradle the back of my head, encouraging me to hide my face in his neck.

Excellent idea. How the hell did he tolerate people getting all up in his grill all of the time? Outside his home, for heaven's sake.

Small point: I could ignore the heat and scent of him while avoiding appearing on gossip sites no problem whatsoever. Women are multitasking masters at the best of times. Achieving both of these aims at once would not be a problem at all. Even if nibbling on his shoulder had once been a favorite hobby of mine. That I wanted to sexually attack him in the middle of a press and fan frenzy was disturbing news.

My hands clutched at him, holding on tightly as he strode into an upscale apartment building. The shouting voices and flashing lights faded behind us, the concrete walkway changing to a smooth marble floor.

"Evening, Mr. Dillon," said the concierge, an attractive older woman with grey hair drawn back in a neat bun. She didn't even take a second glance at me clinging to the man like a howler monkey. Dignity certainly played no part in my current position. I guessed in an apartment building like this, they saw all sorts of things. Because this had to be the infamous building where half of the world-famous band Stage Dive lived. The rock band who'd given Adam a hand-up in the music world after I'd kicked him out.

The tears slowed, though my breath still came in hiccupping sobs. How embarrassing. So not okay. His sneakers squeaked against the white marble flooring as Bon the bodyguard pushed the button for the elevator. All in all, the apartment building seemed to be some art-deco throwback with lots of shiny surfaces. A couple of pieces of expensive art stood on pedestals. The overall effect was one of expense and privilege.

"You can put me down now," I said, doing my best to sound calm, cool, and collected. "Thank you."

Adam frowned, but did as asked. His hands gripped my waist as I slid down his long, hard body. The whole experience made me tingle in a most unwelcome way. We were broken up. Way broken up. Tonight had turned all too emotional and physical for some reason. Not what I'd planned at all. Hard nipples poked at the thin material of my blue cropped tee, and my stomach flip-flopped. I crossed my arms over my chest and focused on my breathing. Everything would be fine. Denial was ace.

When the elevator arrived, a couple was already standing inside, having obviously come up from the parking level beneath the building.

The dude with long blond hair and tattoos had a baby attached to his front in one of those infant carriers. A pretty redhaired woman stood next to him, carting a baby bag. It was black with little cartoon skulls on it. So much rock 'n' roll cool with diapers included.

"Adam. Dude, bro," said the man. "How's it hanging?"

"Hey, Adam, Bon." The woman gave me a somewhat tired but curious smile. "Hi."

"Anne. Mal." My ex nodded and said no more. He definitely didn't introduce me. Even more awkward.

Bon pressed the button for a floor near the top of the building, and off we went.

Meanwhile, if Adam's new rock star status didn't overexcite me, the elevator's current occupants sure did. I mean…holy shit. I may or may not have been a devoted member of the Stage Dive fan club for several years. David Ferris remained my favorite. Which actually might explain my whole tall, tattooed, long dark-haired guitarist fascination, now that I thought about it. But back to the famous dude who stared me in the face.

"Who's your friend?" asked Mal. As in Malcolm Ericson, the drummer for Stage Dive. "The girl currently ogling me with slack-jawed wonder. Her eyes are red. Did you upset her?"

I shut my mouth and turned away. Gawky tweens showed more cool than I currently exhibited. With ease.

Mal played with a tiny socked foot that was sticking out of the baby sling. "It's okay. Don't be embarrassed. I am indeed amazing. Why the things I can do would frankly astound you. Take this infant attached to my chest here…his name is Tommy. I made him."

The pretty redhead, Anne, shook her head. "If memory serves, I think you might have had some help with that."

"Geez, babe, you're as bad as Davie. Remember when he wanted co-writer credits on *Fall* for just filling in the gaps between my drum fills?"

"Filling in the gaps with stuff like lyrics and music, you mean?" asked Anne. How the woman managed to keep a straight face was beyond me.

"Exactly. The little stuff. But no…apparently, you just have to be in the room when the magic is happening and you get co-writer credits. It's a good thing I'm so magnanimous about sharing the glory." Mal stopped for a moment and looked between Adam and me as if a thought had just struck him. "Young Adam, when Davie allowed you to purchase an apartment in his building, there were certain stipulations attached to the sale. And one of those, as you well know, is no female friends are allowed to visit. You're much too young and foolish. As evidenced by the fact that you've already somehow managed to mess up and make her cry. Shame on you."

"I thought the lower garage was out of action," grumbled Adam.

"For everyone else, yes," said Mal. "But it takes more than a parking gate to stop me. Ever since Sam started to share his cool commando spy tips, I've been unstoppable."

"By spy tips, you mean whining until the super gave you the emergency override codes?" asked Anne without even a hint of sarcasm. What a woman.

The elevator chimed and slid to a stop. Bon stepped out and put his hand over the door opening to stop it from closing. Adam grabbed my hand and followed, tugging me along.

"Let's not change the subject from Adam's misdeeds," continued Mal in a low voice so as not to wake the sleeping baby. "I'm sorry, boy, but you know it's for your own good. Also, it's past your bedtime. Don't forget to brush your teeth first though."

"He's about the same age as you were when we met," said Anne.

"Yeah, but drummers mature faster than guitarists. Everyone knows that, pumpkin." Mal sighed. "Adam, you're just not emotionally mature enough to deal with sexual intimacy and adult relationships. Not sure you ever will be. Take my advice and stick to the hand. I appreciate that this is the first time you've attempted to bring a lady friend home—that I'm aware of. Which makes me even more curious about just who she is. But the rule still stands. Send the nice girl on her way, please."

We stood in another hallway with doors leading to apartments at either end. More white marble on the floor. This place must cost a small fortune, and Adam lived here now. Yikes.

Adam turned back and stared at the drummer.

Mal tipped his chin. "What?"

Anne waved at one and all. "Ignore my idiot husband and have a nice night."

Without comment, Bon removed his hand, and the elevator doors started to close.

Then Mal grinned. He grinned like a man who found himself immensely amusing. I had to admit, he was kind of funny. "Mystery girl is smiling," said Mal. "She likes me!"

His wife shushed him. "You'll wake Tommy."

"Sorry, sorry." His voice dropped to a conspiratorial whisper. "By the way, it's not called 'whining' when spies do it. It's 'working an asset.'"

And then they were gone.

"I'm not sure if he's different than how I thought he'd be, or exactly how I thought he'd be." I frowned in thought. "You live with actual rock stars. Wow."

Adam frowned in annoyance. "I am a rock star."

"Eh."

"At least he got you to stop crying."

Bon opened the apartment door and dealt with the security system before looking back to Adam with some unspoken request. Sure enough, he took over holding open the door so the bodyguard could move into the apartment, turning on lights as he went. There were wide wooden floorboards, tall arched windows, and an interesting color scheme. A long, pale blue plush-looking sofa, a grey rug, and a couple of white leather armchairs. A silver resonator guitar hung on the wall along with a collection of gold and platinum albums. The rest of his guitars would be somewhere close. Even before all of the money, he'd owned a minimum of three or four at any given time, including a Martin he'd won in a poker game. And then there were the amps, a veritable wall of them. Old valve amps that looked like they dated back to the ark, and gleaming new ones with enough buttons and knobs to intimidate an air traffic controller. It was a wonder we could move about in the tiny living room at my place with all of his stuff. For certain, he wouldn't have the same issue here. The apartment was huge.

"How many records did you have to sell to get those?" I asked, looking at the framed records.

"Half a million for the gold, and a million for the platinum."

"No wonder so many people try to friend me on social media to discuss you and how I ruined our perfect relationship."

His brows went up. "People do that?"

"Yep."

"I never told anyone your name."

"Word got around anyway."

The man did not look happy. He slipped a hand to my lower back, urging me into the apartment. "Bon will be finished with his security check in a minute. Come on in."

"Has anyone ever actually been hiding out in your shower or under your bed?"

He shook his head, tucking his straggly long hair behind his ears. "This building's secure. It's why I bought the place. Along with Dave and Mal being here already."

"You're close to them, huh?"

"They've been good friends. Most of the time." He glanced over at me, his forehead furrowed.

"What? What is that look for?"

"Nothing." He paused. "It's just strange seeing you again. You in this context is…interesting. Not bad, just unexpected."

"Tell me about it."

"I thought you hated me."

My shoulders slumped. "Ignore what I said in the car. I was having a very small and probably long-overdue meltdown. But the truth is, I never hated you. It probably would have been easier if I had.

You just disappointed me, big time."

Bon wandered out of one of the back rooms, standing almost at attention. "Will you be in for the rest of the night, Mr. Dillon?"

"Yeah, I'll stay put. Don't worry. You can head home." From out of the glossy double fridge, Adam retrieved two beers and set them on the white stone countertop. The rest of the kitchen was navy. Very dramatic.

On silent feet, Bon exited the apartment, locking the front door behind him.

"This sure is a change from my crappy little apartment." I took the beer he offered, taking a long gulp. My throat was still itchy from the totally unnecessary tears. "You must love it here."

He shrugged.

"Did you buy it already decorated?"

"Yeah. Some financier asshole lived here last." He sprawled out on the white couch. "Pretty sure Mal annoyed the dude into moving. None of them liked him. Apparently, he complained about the bodyguards coming and going, the fans out front, and all that."

"Guess it would take some getting used to."

He took a swig of his beer.

"Are we going to talk about the check?" I asked, slipping into one of the armchairs. Very comfy. "I think we should."

"What's there to say? You deserve the money, Jill. As far as I'm concerned, you earned it."

"Adam—"

"No one supported me and my music like you did. Showing up for every gig you could, helping to lug equipment, giving me space to write my songs." He stared out a window at the lights of the Pearl District. "Even if it was too much for you in the end..."

I downed some beer. The less said about ye olde days, the better. It would only lead to more fights. And what was even the point of rehashing the past yet again?

His sneaker tapped out a beat against the floor and he pulled out his cell. Soon enough, *Howlin' Wolf* played over the sound system.

Blues had always been his go-to when stressed. "Too damn quiet in here."

"Is that why you go out all the time?" I crossed my legs, waving my foot in the air. Guess we were both a little wired. "Heard Martha say something about it when you got in the car. And then there's the tea being served in mighty amounts. Did you really trash a hotel room? Isn't that a bit clichéd?"

"Everything worth doing eventually becomes a cliché." He put the beer to his lips again. "So you *are* keeping tabs on me."

"I don't need to. Certain people are only too happy to tell me everything and anything when it comes to you." I stared at the wall. "You should have seen the messages I received when you were photographed with that model, Mae Cooper."

He snorted. "She's a neighbor."

"How handy."

"She's also engaged to Bon's brother. Who's almost as intimidating as Bon is. Not a family you want to mess with."

I paused. "Oh."

He just watched me.

"What?" I snapped.

A small amused smile curled his lips. "Not like you to be jealous."

"Go fuck yourself." I set my beer and the check down on the coffee table, hauled my ass out of the chair and made for the door. Stupid. I was so breathtakingly stupid. With a bit of work, I could have found an address for Martha and just mailed the damn money to her. She'd have passed it on to him. But no. I had to see the big jerkwad for myself. "This is getting us nowhere. I never should have come."

My fingers no sooner gripped the doorknob than he was there, hands flat against the front door, blocking my exit. I looked up and growled. "Move, Adam."

"Go pick up the check."

"I don't want your money."

"Yes, you do. You dumped me over money."

I shook my head. "That was only part of it. A very small part of it.

The straw that broke the camel's back, so to speak. Now move."

"We're not done talking."

"Oh yes we are. Unless of course you'd like to get punched in the dick."

His gaze hardened. "I'm sorry, all right? I'm sorry. Is that what you want to hear?"

"Move!"

With a snarl of his own, he took a step back, frustration etched into his handsome face. "Fuck's sake, Jill. Why do you always have to be so…?"

"So, what?"

He just shook his head, mouth tight with frustration.

"Go on. Say it."

"Emotional," he spat. "It's always pushing with you. Where's our relationship heading? What are my plans for the future? How do I feel about you? We could never just fucking be. The crazy thing is, I was with you. I was a hundred and ten percent with you and it still wasn't enough."

"Maybe you should have told me that instead of mumbling excuses when I needed to talk."

He shook his head.

"Anyway, got some amazing news for you, Adam. We're no longer together. You no longer have to tolerate my needy, chatty ass." I wrenched open the door, paused, and slammed it shut again. If this was the last time I ever saw the jerk, then I would say everything I needed to say. And I'd say it now, right up nice and close to his face in a nice clear angry voice. "But while I'm here, how fucking dare you? You wrote a whole damn album telling the world how you felt when you couldn't even tell me. Not once. Not even once did you tell me how you felt about me."

"You kicked me out."

"You took me for granted."

"You blocked my number."

"You behaved like an emotionally repressed immature asshole, and I didn't want to talk to you." I slammed my hands against his chest. "So there," I yelled like a reasonable adult.

"I loved you!" he roared back at me. "I loved you, Jill. And maybe I was shit at showing it, but I would have figured it out. I would have gotten there. Why the hell did you give up on me so soon?"

I stared at him, stunned. The blood drained out of my face, my brain feeling both light and heavy at the same time. "You did? You mean that? You really loved me?"

"Of course, I did," he said, shoulders falling, the fight leaching out of the man. "And it's not like you ever said it to me either."

Huh.

"Was it that asshole Chris who was always hanging around?"

"What?" I shook my head, trying to think straight. "No. There was no one else."

"Bet he was knocking on your door not five minutes after you threw me out." He cracked his knuckles all Neanderthal-like. "The way he used to look at you…"

Holy cow. Adam had loved me. I'd thought it was all some bad joke or publicity stunt. An artistic temperament leading to imagined feelings or something similar. But he'd actually finally said the words, and from what I could tell, he meant them. Guess still waters really did run deep. And I'd never said it to him because everyone knew the guy had to say it first. It was like an unwritten rule. Still, this new information had my heart hammering inside my chest. "Chris? Really? He does absolutely nothing for me. Never has. Guess I'm not the only one with jealousy issues."

"Guess not." A muscle popped on the side of his jaw. Then he squeezed his eyes shut, sucking in a deep breath and letting it out slowly. "What the hell are we doing? Can we not fight for a while? Is that even possible?"

"I don't know."

Silence.

Neither of us seemed to know what to say. And the quiet was neither easy nor comfortable. My head was reeling, and even Adam seemed sort of dazed. We'd had the odd disagreement before the big this-is-the-end-of-us moment that led to me kicking him out. However, we'd never yelled in each other's faces quite like that before. Maybe we should have. More than a little honesty seemed to have slipped out along with all of the accusations and anger.

"Mae is a neighbor and a friend. Nothing more." He finally turned and headed back to the sofa. "Would have thought you'd have replaced me by now for sure, though."

"I haven't really been in the mood for dating."

"For a year?"

I shrugged. My dry spell didn't need to be discussed.

Once more, he sprawled on the couch, finished off the beer. Eyes closed, he laid his head back against the cushions.

"What about you?" I asked, voice lowered. I could have left. I probably should have, given it would have been the smart thing to do. Yet my feet stayed still. No one had ever told me they loved me before outside of family, who were basically obligated to say that sort of thing. No one had given me that and meant it. It was a little overwhelming.

"What about me? You mean dating?" he asked, eyes still closed. "Nah. Not in the right headspace, besides being too busy recording and touring. The promo appearances alone have been never-ending."

I stood behind the wingback, hands resting on top. "You look exhausted, and you stink."

"You always said you liked the way I smelled."

No way would I be going near that. "If you're so damn tired, why were you heading to a club?"

"So I could play on the down-low with some local musicians. Just hang out and relax. Have a couple of beers and unwind without a whole lot of fuss."

"No partying with groupies, huh?"

"Sad to say, but after you sign the first couple pairs of tits, it kind of loses its thrill. Mal was right about that. Of course, if he tried to sign any these days, Anne would chop off his hands." He chuckled. "Too much drinking and my playing started to suffer so I had to cut back.

Martha got Jimmy to give me a talking to after the hotel room incident."

"Jimmy Ferris?"

"The one and only. Lead singer of Stage Dive and reformed addict." He sighed, a soul-deep kind of noise. "What he had to say scared the shit out of me, actually. Lots of people offer you all sorts of things when you get big. Not that I'm as big as them. But the champagne just flows, let alone the hard stuff. I could have easily been headed straight for the 27 Club. He talked some sense into me, and I slowed it down."

"Good. I know I used to ride you about sleeping half the day away, but you looked better back then. You looked—" *Beautiful.* I almost said it. "Healthy. Alive."

He grunted. Some habits hadn't changed. At least, not entirely. Overhead, the air-conditioning clicked on, the quiet hum the only sound since the song had finished. Not a single noise from the city filtered through. One of Adam's eyes opened, taking me in.

I rested my arms against the top of the chair. "What?"

"Just checking you're still here," he replied.

"I wouldn't leave without saying something."

"Will you stay awhile? Please?" His eyelids fluttered and then fell closed again. "Despite the arguing, it's good having you here."

"Are you okay? You look totally shot."

"No, I'm fine. It's always like this after a show. Just stay awhile, okay?"

I hesitated. Of course, I did. But in the end, I couldn't say no. He was so obviously rundown and lonely in this crazy new life of his. And we probably needed to argue some more about the check. There was that to be considered. "Okay."

I sat down on the couch, curling my feet under me. Not so far away that I was being distant but not so near that either of us might find the other's physical presence distracting. God knew how often I used to find his body distracting. Vexingly, impossibly, wonderfully distracting.

Adam gave a slight nod, his eyes still shut. Then his body relaxed fully against the couch. Within minutes, he was asleep. Adam had always been able to drop off easily while I tossed and turned and pondered something completely stupid and unnecessary for an hour or so. Like why dresses rarely had pockets (so they could sell us handbags) and if penguins ever got cold and wanted to move to the Bahamas. Important life-altering stuff. But even Adam had never fallen asleep this fast. How damn tired must the man be? In and out, in and out, his easy breathing filled the room. The number of nights that sound had lulled me to sleep, safe in the knowledge he was there. The one person who could turn me inside out with a single look.

And he'd left me alone in his lux new apartment where I definitely did not belong.

"Holy shit," I whispered. "Now what do I do?"

Chapter Three

Of course, I had to have a snoop around. No way could I waste this opportunity to intrude upon his space and spy on his new life.

Farther back in the apartment sat his large bedroom, walk-in wardrobe, and bathroom all done up in gray. At most, he'd filled up maybe a tenth of the wardrobe with a variety of jeans, including ripped and non-ripped, black and various shades of blue. A stack of tees and hoodies. A dozen or so pairs of shoes including sneakers and boots. His old battered leather jacket and a couple of flannel and button-down shirts. Not much had changed. Despite the gorgeous suit I'd seen him wearing on a magazine cover accepting a music award (the shirt's crisp arrow collar juxtaposed nicely with his stubble, tousled hair and devil-may-care smile), he obviously hadn't given in to a stylist for his everyday wear. In one corner sat a large stack of unopened boxes, but that was about all. In the fancy two-person shower sat a bottle of two-in-one shampoo and conditioner and a crumb of soap. It didn't even look like the ginormous hot tub had ever been used. Make no mistake, I'd have been in there the first chance I got. Wealth was wasted on Adam.

The California-king-size bed sat unmade with pillows that smelled of him and no one else. Which was interesting. Guess he really didn't bring other women back here. Or at least, not recently. And while I probably should have been ashamed of sniffing his belongings, I hadn't reached that stage of the proceedings just yet. I was quite content to suffer pangs of guilt for my appalling behavior, but not until I'd investigated the whole apartment. Priorities mattered. Next were two spare rooms. The first sat empty and the second had been stuffed full of about a dozen guitars and various amps. They lined the walls, just waiting to be played. A notebook and pen were discarded on the floor. As tempting as it was to read what songs he was working on, I managed to respect his privacy and not look.

It kind of evened out the weirdo sniffing thing in my mind.

A half-bathroom and coat closet near the door finished up the apartment. And Adam was still asleep. I threw a blanket over him in case he got cold and headed for the kitchen.

Not a whole heck of a lot in the fridge. Some wilted salad mix, a couple of pieces of pizza, a variety of beer, a block of cheese, some orange juice, a bit of butter, and milk. Cold cuts turning a suspicious shade of green, and bread more than a few days old. Those went in the trash. If I was overstepping, he could get mad at me later. Guess he didn't have a housekeeper. Or at least, not a regular one. The pantry wasn't much better, but I could scrape together mac and cheese— happily one of his favorite comfort foods. I was more of a taco girl myself. Let every day be Taco Tuesday and I'd be happy. Cooking also gave me something to do while he caught up on his sleep. To be honest, being a domestic goddess had never been my thing. Ordering delivery was more my style these days. Didn't mean I couldn't look after him a little this one last time. Because this had to be the last time we'd see each other. My feelings were too confused to allow us to be friends, and he'd be off on tour in a few days' time anyway.

The end was definitely nigh. Not exactly sure how I felt about that.

When he woke, I was humming under my breath to a song by The Nationals, stirring the noodles and sauce together. "That smells good."

"Hey…yeah…I hope you're hungry."

He smiled, and I didn't know what to do. My insides lurched in the strangest way. Me being here was beyond awkward. Us being together. So much was different, yet so much felt the same. Give or take the million-plus-dollar apartment.

"I've been thinking about the check," I said, stopping to take a sip of water.

Adam rose from the couch, stretching so that his tee crept up, revealing a slice of flat stomach and slim hips. The man could eat whatever he wanted while my ass expanded if I so much as looked at a piece of cake. Talk about unfair. Though it didn't stop me from eating cake because happiness mattered more than butt size.

He stood on the opposite side of the counter, staring at me sleepily. "What are you thinking, Jill?"

"Oh. Right. Take one of the zeros off and I'll accept it. I'll give half of the money to a local foodbank and use the rest to get caught up on things. Like replacing my crappy old car and taking a vacation maybe…stuff like that."

Elbows on the stone, he leaned forward, his mess of dark hair falling in his face. Hiding or thinking or a bit of both. "That's a nice idea, though I do support lots of local charities already. Thought you might want to buy your own place. Open your own salon or something."

"Speaking of which, when was the last time you had a haircut?"

"I dunno. Whenever you did it last."

My brows rose as I dished up a bowl of comfort food. "Don't you have stylists and people like that making suggestions about how you look?"

"They suggest. I ignore." He shrugged, sliding onto a stool. "Unless it's for something important, then Martha gets on my case and it's just easier to give in. But I've pretty much just been tying my hair back and ignoring it."

I pushed the bowl across to him, along with a fork.

"You're frowning," he said around a mouthful of food. "This is great. Thanks."

"I'd cut it for you, but I didn't bring my shears. I thought it wise not to bring sharp metal blades to our little catch-up."

He looked up, gaze still tired. Still waking up from his nap. Then he pulled his cell out of his back jeans' pocket and fired off a text. "That's easy enough fixed. Martha will know someone who has a pair."

"Martha is terrifying." I filled my own bowl and started eating. Hot cheesy carb-loaded goodness. Not bad at all.

"I know, right?" He smiled. "This really is good. Thanks."

I nodded. "That why you chose her? Because she scares small children?"

"Small children actually love her. Well...some do." He loaded up his fork. "I chose her because she's honest, if a little blunt. Negotiates contracts down to the last letter. And she doesn't let anyone fuck with me. Not even me."

I finished chewing my mouthful. "Why do you think she let me past the bodyguards and everything?"

"Dunno." He stared off at nothing, seeming to think it over. "There's messing with people, then there's just having a little fun. Putting you and me together might have been her idea of fun."

"Hmm."

"Also a good way to stop me from hanging at any bars tonight. She doesn't like how I've been spending my spare time—not that I get much of it. But better winding down in a bar with music and people than just being alone here."

I stirred my fork around and around, making patterns in the pasta and cheese. "Strange to think you spent so much money on this place but you don't like being here."

"I didn't say that." His shoulders hunched defensively. "Just that it gets a bit quiet. Never lived on my own before. When I was staying at Ben's—"

"The bass player from Stage Dive?" I asked, somewhat awed.

"Yeah. He and his wife are good people. At the house, there was always someone around willing to hang out or jam. Before that, I was coming home to you so...and no, I wasn't with you just so I wouldn't be alone."

"I wasn't thinking that."

"Hmm."

"You can't knock on your friends' doors? The ones that live here?"

He downed a swig of beer. "Feels like intruding on their privacy or something, you know? Everyone's busy as hell. I don't want to interrupt the time they get with their significant others."

"I can see that. Still, these new friends of yours are complex."

"They're just like any other family."

"With the exception of being crazy rich and famous."

"True," he said.

"Is that what they are to you? Family?"

He stabbed at some noodles in a contemplative fashion. "Yeah. I guess they are. They kind of took me in, you know?"

"After I threw you out."

At this, he said nothing. A whole heaping lot of it. Then he cleared his throat. "Maybe I sort of deserved that, you kicking me out and everything."

"Sort of?"

"Alright, so I did deserve it. I got complacent, fixated on the music and forgot about everything else. Well, I didn't forget. I just stopped putting the work in…"

Someone knocked at the front door.

Still avoiding my gaze, Adam stood and ambled on over. Standing outside was a drop-dead-gorgeous buxom woman in a skintight black leather sheath with Louboutin point-toe booties I'd kill for. Seriously. What was it with these women and amazing footwear?

Which was about when I realized that the woman standing in the doorway was supermodel Mae Cooper. It would be nice to say I didn't stare all bedazzled-like. But that would be a lie. She was magnificent with curves for days and perfect skin. Given sufficient time to adjust to being in the presence of yet another famous person, I'd definitely have grilled her about her skincare routine.

"Martha said you needed these?" She handed a pair of scissors to Adam before giving me a smile, accompanied by a curious look. "Hi, you must be Jill. Nice to meet you." She pointed guiltily at the scissors. "Don't think badly of me, but I have been known to tamper with my own hair from time to time."

"It happens," I answered, sounding stilted. "Oh, umm…hi."

"My stylist goes off at me every time. He almost burst into tears the time I cut myself bangs. Honestly, you'd think I'd learn."

My brain wouldn't work, so I said nothing.

"Starstruck again," muttered Adam. "Incredible."

"Oh dear, that sounds like jealousy. Isn't she finding you sufficiently impressive?" Mae grinned. "They can't all fall at your feet, Adam. It would get boring."

He frowned. "With her, just once would be nice."

"Best of luck with that." Mae patted him on the cheek and disappeared.

Adam closed the door with a frown.

"Any other famous people going to appear?" I asked, stirring my fork through the midnight meal. "If so, I kind of need time to mentally prepare myself."

"I hope not." He sat down once more, heaping his fork. "You know they're just normal people with high-profile jobs, right?"

"Yes, but they have that famous-people thing about them."

He raised a brow. "In that case, don't I have that thing?"

"No," I said. "I've lived with you. You are neither glossy and lit from within nor mysterious and otherworldly. Like Mae. Or Mal, even if he is crazy."

"The only thing mysterious about Mal is how someone hasn't snapped and killed him yet."

I laughed.

We ate in silence for a while, the scissors sitting on the counter between us like both a promise and a threat. Maybe I shouldn't have offered to cut his hair, despite it badly needing a trim and then some. Cutting hair was my job, but it still involved touching. Not always pleasant, but not usually something that resulted in an existential crisis on my part. Normally the touching component wasn't something I gave a great deal of thought to, due to having a professional attitude, etcetera. However, I wasn't certain I should be getting within six feet of this particular male. And yet, on the other hand, I couldn't help but feel a smidgeon of proprietary attachment to both the man and his hair. God, this was complicated. Feelings were the worst.

"What?" he asked with a raised brow, the bowl of food in front of him already almost empty. He started gathering up the dirty plates and putting them into the sink. The leftovers went into the fridge. A nice show of newfound domestic abilities.

"Finish up and I'll do your hair, then I better get going."

"You want to leave?"

"You want me to stay?"

"I already said as much."

I licked my lips. "Thought you just meant for an hour or two, not the night."

He lifted one shoulder in a shrug.

As if that told me anything. Ugh. And then a random and slightly scary thought occurred to me. I stood tall and raised my chin. "I'm not sleeping with you."

"You're not, huh?"

"Nope."

"I find it interesting that that was where your mind went, because who said anything about sex?" It was like the word *sex* hung in the hair between us, his tone of voice a dare. If he hadn't been thinking about it before then, he sure as hell was now. "Maybe you missed me more than you're letting on."

No wonder I couldn't find my balance with him. He switched from seemingly sweet and innocent to blatant and porny in the blink of an eye. His gaze darkened and he stared me down, taking me in with seemingly infinite patience. And there was such intimacy in his eyes. Such knowledge of me and us and every damn thing we'd ever done together. Because irrespective of everything else that hadn't worked in our relationship, the sex had always worked. Despite the heat in my cheeks, I couldn't have looked away if I tried. Next, a shiver worked its way down my spine, every inch of me suddenly hyper-aware of the skin I was in. Of the heaviness in my breasts and ache between my legs. Stupid hormones and body.

For so damn long, the male race in its entirety had left me cold and unmoved. After getting my heart smashed, it had been a bit of a relief to take a break. But now…how could I have forgotten?

Talk about unfair. The man was beautiful.

I swallowed hard. "Stop it."

"Stop what?"

"You're staring."

"So are you." Then he smiled as if something had been decided. I did not trust that smile. It was a sly sort of thing, suggesting he remembered full well what I looked like naked but wouldn't mind a refresher if I'd be so kind as to disrobe. Damn him and his heated looks. I did not need this sort of confusion in my life.

"Fine," I said with way too much going on inside me. "Whatever. As long as you know nothing is happening between us. I'm not here for anything like that. Just to cut the split ends off your hair and shave a zero off that check. That's all."

"Okay," he said, face a careful blank.

"Great. Glad we got that sorted."

"You know what I just realized?" he asked, standing and pulling his tee over his head. Just getting half-naked as if that were in any way acceptable and flashing the upper half of his lean hard body at me. The bastard. All of his ink and smooth skin and…oh my God I was melting inside. At this rate I'd be a puddle of girl goo in no time.

"What are you doing?" I squeaked.

"Don't want hair stuck in my shirt." He pushed his hair back from his face and dragged the barstool away from the counter into an open space. "This do?"

"Yeah. I'll need a brush and comb too."

He wandered off toward the bathroom, retrieving the requested items. Then he sat down and patiently waited. Still half-naked, dammit. "I was telling you about the moment I just had."

And I was seriously not certain I wanted to know.

"That being defensive and in denial isn't going to get us anywhere."

I sniffed. "Speak for yourself. I have no plans to get myself anywhere anyway."

"Think about it. This is a chance for us to clear the air. To maybe get things sorted between us. Get on the road to being friends, if that's what you want."

Oh no. Hell no. Being Adam's buddy sure as hell wasn't in the cards. My fake smile couldn't possibly stand up to seeing him with another woman. Not that I'd be saying that out loud anytime this century.

"Things are sorted. They have been for a long time. Are you sure you trust me around you with sharp objects?" I asked, mostly joking. Like, ninety-nine percent.

"I trust you just fine."

No comment from me. I picked up the shears, testing out their motion. Mae certainly hadn't scrimped on quality. They were professional-level. With the scissors back on the bench, I took up the brush and started in on his tangles. No big deal. Just doing my job. Nothing special about touching him and being all up in his face at all. If my fingers hesitated a moment before making contact…it was just one of those things. The weirdness of exes and so on.

There'd been no lie when he said I liked how he smelled. Getting closer only amped it up more. Hard not to take a few nice deep breaths. At this range, the faint spicy hint of his aftershave lotion became detectable. Something expensive, no doubt. In all likelihood, my reaction to him could be labeled the comfort of familiarity. He'd been the great love of my life up until now, but others would come, and I'd eventually move on. Some of them might even end up better in bed than Adam. You never knew. Miracles did happen.

He reached for his phone, putting on some old Fleetwood Mac.

One of my favorites.

Meanwhile, I carefully brushed out his hair, ignoring the heat of his skin and the width of his shoulders because…I was a boss like that. "You should take better care of it. Two-in-one shampoo is lazy-ass nonsense and you know it."

"You had a nose-around, huh?"

"Nope. Lucky guess, that's all."

He was smart enough not to fall for that. "Looking for anything in particular?"

I sighed. "No. Just looking."

"Right." He chuckled. "Can't believe you haven't been on even one date in the last year."

"Can't believe you're making a big deal out of it." I exchanged the brush for the comb. "If I want company, I have friends. If I feel the need to get laid, I can organize that without too much difficulty as well. I just wasn't in the mood. Stop reading so much into it."

"I know. I'm well aware you don't need anyone just for the sake of having someone," he said. "But you were a great girlfriend. Partner. Whatever you want to call it. Seems a shame you're not interested in sharing your life with someone special, you know?"

I sighed. "I'm just going to say thank you, and we're going to stop this line of questioning, okay?"

A nod from him.

"A couple of inches off sound good?"

"Whatever you think is best."

So I started cutting, stopping to brush hair off his back and shoulders as I went. Nothing special about skimming my fingers across his warm skin time and again. Nothing remarkable about the way he silently watched me as I worked on his front. Even if his gaze did ever so slightly unnerve me. The way he took in my eyes, my mouth, and the line of my neck leading down to my chest. The way the little hairs on his body stood on end, and so did mine. Guess we both got to each other. We always had.

I didn't rush the job, but I didn't mess around either.

"Take one of the zeros off the check," I prodded when the silence had stretched too long.

"No."

"Stop being difficult or we're never going to reach an agreement."

"You earned the money. Keep it." His voice was low and quiet. Determined. "I want you to have it."

I frowned. And then I paused, taking his face in my hand and inspecting his stubbled jawline. The pad of my thumb ran back and forth over a small pink indentation. "What is this? How did you get this scar?"

"Someone threw a chunky silver ring at me at a festival about six months back. I think it was meant to be a gift."

"Hell of a gift."

"Just bad luck." He reached up and gave my hand a squeeze. "Don't worry about it."

"I thought you had security."

"They can't be everywhere all the time. Things happen." A sweet slow smile curled his lips. "Jill, baby, I'm fine. It's just rock and roll. No need to get angry."

"I'm not angry." Mildly outraged he'd been harmed, but not angry.

"Then stop scowling, you're scaring me to death."

"Very funny." With a deep breath, I relaxed my face and channeled some nice calm thoughts. "People shouldn't be throwing things at you. It's rude and dangerous."

"Usually it's just panties, flowers—soft stuff like that."

"Ew."

His smile amped up and he was back to staring. God I liked that way more than I wanted to admit. But he had to know. What with the way I kept meeting his gaze before looking away, acting all nervous and on edge.

Finally, he licked his lips. "You wouldn't believe how many times I thought about picking up the phone to call you. Wanting to tell you about something that had happened. Then I'd remember...you didn't want to talk to me."

"Like you weren't mad at me too."

"Oh, I was. For a week or two. Then I just felt like an ass more than anything."

"So, what? You wrote that whole album during the week or two you were angry at me?"

"Yeah. Basically. Channeled everything into the music. Worked through it all and realized I was wrong, and you were right." He watched me with a raised brow. "But the songs were good. It wasn't like I was going to let them go to waste and not play them."

"Of course not." I snorted and set down the scissors. "Say it again, the *I was right and you were wrong* part."

"I was right, and you were wrong."

I growled and launched myself at him, putting much energy into messing up his now nice and neat hair, making it fall all over his stupid handsome face, sprinkling tiny snippets of cut hair all over us, like so much confetti. "You're done, Adam. In all the ways."

"Wait, wait, wait." He grabbed my hips, grinning all the while. "I was wrong. You were right. There...I said it."

"Again."

All amused-like, he looked skyward. "You're a demanding woman. You know that?"

"Damn right I am."

"Damn right you are."

Impossible not to smile back at him. Lord, I was a weak-willed woman. His fingers flexed, digging into the flesh of my hips just a little, and perhaps Adam still felt a touch possessive about me and my body too.

He slipped a hand behind my ear, gentle as can be. "I like the silver hair."

"Thanks." We were whispering for some reason.

For the longest time, he just kept staring at me. It was as if we were both hypnotized by the sight of the other. Neither of us could stop. His hand lingered on the side of my head before slipping around to embrace the back of my neck and urge me forward. Pulling me closer. And I couldn't *not* taste him. My mouth watered at just the thought.

"Adam..."

"I'm right here."

Which was kind of both the good part and the problem.

He ushered my body between his spread legs and our mouths were on exactly the right trajectory for impact. One. Two. Three. Bam. We were kissing. Lips pressing softly together at first before the hunger grew. It was all so familiar and right. Easy, even. With one hand grabbing the back of my neck just how I liked it and the other beneath my tee, sliding over the skin of my back, the man kissed me hard and sure. His tongue slid against mine. His teeth nipped at my bottom lip.

My head spun and my knees went weak. My blood boiled inside my veins. I wanted everything and I wanted it now. So much for not sleeping with him. If this didn't end in an orgasm, there'd be hell to pay. I needed it so badly. And not just from anyone, it had to be from him.

I'd forgotten how well we fit together. How perfect his mouth was against mine. Way back when we'd been together, he'd made a study of how to please me physically for both the right and wrong reasons. Adam loved working things out in bed, and I had to admit...I didn't mind it either. Sex to get my mind off the mess he'd made. Sex to distract me from our money situation. Or yes, even sex just to see me smile. And he hadn't forgotten a damn thing. If only he'd used his powers for good instead of evil, we might still be together.

His firm wet lips fed me kiss after kiss as his hard thighs clamped shut on my hips (as if I were going anywhere). Stepping back from him, pulling away had never even crossed my mind. That's the honest truth. All of the heat inside of me had roared back to life at his touch. My body had been asleep for so long. Instead of doing the sensible thing, I fisted my hands in his hair and gave as good as I got. Biting and licking and demanding more.

A growl rumbled up from deep in his throat and his hands shifted, changing position to attack the button and zipper of my jeans. It was like the item of clothing personally offended him or something. Had done him wrong.

"Shoes," I panted.

"Shit."

Again, his hands moved, cupping my ass cheeks, lifting me off my feet and depositing me on the kitchen counter. Slashes of pink highlighted his cheekbones. With nil preamble, he tore into the laces on my boots, wresting the shoes and socks from my feet. Next came my jeans. This was the benefit of him being bigger and me being smaller. In times of duress, he could just lift and maneuver me as required. It was time effective if nothing else.

The nice thing about screwing around with an ex was the lack of physical angst. He'd seen my body many times before. Knew my ass wobbled a little and that my breasts were small. For certain, there was no performance anxiety or fear of him finding the dimples on my thighs off-putting. So that was a bonus. It should also be noted that guitarists' hands are mighty swift and sure. A pair of panties went flying over his shoulder and my tee and bra weren't far behind. I sat bare-assed on the cool stone counter.

Then he paused. "Do I need—?"

"No." I shook my head. "Not for my sake. What about you?"

"Haven't done anything unprotected and I was tested recently."

Truth be told, I kind of wanted to slap him for breaking our unspoken yearlong no-sex ban. Just because he hadn't known of its existence was no excuse. In all honesty, I felt a little feral right then. A bit violent. Only he made me crazy like this.

A small smile curled his lips at the expression on my face.

"Shut up," I snapped.

"Let me make it up to you."

Strong hands gripped my ankles, lifting and parting them, a move necessitating that my back hit the stone surface. But I didn't protest because I wasn't an idiot. Instead, excitement had my pulse racing, my ribcage tightening. He bussed the insides of my thighs, stubble tickling and scraping against sensitive skin. I didn't know where all of the oxygen in the room had gone. Somewhere important, I hoped. To someone who needed it.

Adam licked and nipped and teased a trail from my knee to where my leg met my body. I both loved and hated how he took his time, making me squirm bare-ass-naked all over, eager-like against the hard surface.

When he finally, at long last, blew a fine stream of air across my wet pussy, I just about came right there and then. His hands wrapped around my thighs, holding me open to his gaze. "Fuck, I missed you."

"Or a certain part of me."

"All of you," he insisted, getting closer but still not getting the job done.

"Adam. Stop messing around."

"So damn impatient."

I shoved my fingers into his hair, holding him down. His answering laughter was all things low and wicked. Sinful and hot and...shit. As the pads of his thumbs held my labia open, he dragged his tongue through the length of me. My hips shot off the counter, grinding against his face. And the man went to town, eating me just how I liked. Lucky this was a hard countertop, because at this rate, some cleanup would be required I was so wet.

With teeth and tongue and lips he went to town on me, working me higher and higher. I had to admit, his delight in oral had long been a plus. He didn't scrimp or get bored halfway through like some guys. Oh, no. Adam made a meal of me on his kitchen counter. My breath came in little pants, and my heart lodged high in my throat. Every inch of me awakened and came alive under his ministrations.

I sucked in a breath. "Fuck."

He made a humming noise and homed in on my clit. We knew each other too damn well. Knew what drove each other crazy and what got us off. Some sucking and flicks of his tongue. A light bite. And I was done. With a loud groan, I came, body tensing, drawing up tight before releasing and rocketing for the stars. Without a doubt, he knew how to send me interstellar. Dammit.

I was still twitching when he picked me up and pushed me up against the nearest appliance.

"We're fucking against the fridge?" I asked, arms and legs wrapped tightly around his body.

"Yep."

"Haven't done that before."

His smile was all teeth.

Then he was pushing into me, the hard length of his cock stretching and claiming me. It was both grueling and delightful for everyone involved. I knew I wasn't the only one who moaned. Adam was nice-sized. A good, decent, not-to-be-ignored sort of size. And he knew what to do with it. Something he was apparently only too pleased to once again prove by drawing out slowly before slamming back in. All of those little muscles inside of me trembled and spasmed around him, welcoming him home.

No. This was just sex. Pure fucking. Nothing more.

Forehead resting against my shoulder, his chest worked furiously to take in air. "Jill. Jesus, baby."

"It feels good," I allowed, voice breathy.

"Yeah." He laughed, looking up at me. In all honesty, he did smell damn good. The scent of fresh sweat on his skin got me high. All of the heat and hardness of him, centered in on me, was arousing as hell.

With no further words, gaze locked on mine, he proceeded to nail me to the fridge. His pupils were dilated, the expression on his face determined. Hips working hard, his dick embedding itself deep inside me with each and every thrust. I'd have bruises tomorrow from the hard grip of his hands. Just how I liked.

And while he might have been trying to prove something, his excitement and vigor was his undoing. With his pelvis working against me, his whole body taut, he growled and came. God, I loved that, feeling his cock jerk inside of me. The way his whole body responded when he came. Eyelids slammed shut, he ground himself against me, finishing with his face hidden in my neck, something he'd done since the first time we were together. Like it was too much, too revealing, too…everything.

"I'm sorry," he eventually said when he'd gotten his breath back.

"You have nothing to be sorry for."

"I wanted to make you come again. Instead I lost it like a goddamn kid."

"You can make me come again later. I'm a giver like that." I chuckled, threading my hands through his hair. Talk about proprietorial. Truth was, once I started touching him, it was damn hard to stop. I ran my fingers over his shoulders, down the length of his spine—or as far as I could reach. Did it need to be mentioned that there wasn't an inch of him I didn't want to touch? Not that it was a big deal or anything. So I might have been behaving in a slightly clingy fashion for a moment, it was just the old post-coital bliss haze. Memories making me maudlin and romantic or something. The allure of feeling close to someone. And I *did* feel close to him. Scarily so. "I need to use the bathroom."

"Right," he said. As if I was made of spun glass, he set my feet gently on the floor. Next, he put himself away and pulled up his jeans. His mouth opened, but for the longest time, no words came out. "There's some um better shampoo and stuff in the cabinet under the sink if you want to have a bath or a shower or…you know."

"There is, huh?"

A nod.

With much awkwardness, we both stood there staring at each other. At the floor. At a wall. It was all greatly fascinating and not a form of avoidance at all. I crossed my hands over my breasts. So stupid given I remained buck-ass naked in my ex's apartment after just having sex.

"Can I come?" he asked.

"You just did."

"I meant can I accompany you to the bathroom or do you want some space?"

In days of yore, we had indeed showered together often after conjugal bliss. And despite it not necessarily feeling like a good idea, us spending more one-on-one time together without our clothes and all, I couldn't actually think of the right way to say as much in the allotted time. "Sure. That's fine. Whatever."

He gave me a look most dubious. But when I about-faced and headed in the direction of the bathroom, he did indeed follow. I could totally feel his eyes on my ass, too. He followed me all the way to the door, where he abruptly halted. "I'll give you your space. You need anything, I'll just be out here."

"Alright."

"Use whatever you want. Make yourself at home."

I nodded.

"I know this is weird. But I want it to be a good weird."

I had no idea what to say to that. Actually, that was a lie. "Was that belated break-up sex?"

"I honestly have no idea." His expression was calm, face relaxed as he seemed to think it over. "Maybe?"

"Right. Okay." And with a little finger wave, I shut the door in his face.

A wise woman who learned from her past mistakes would have been out the door pronto. I apparently was not a wise woman. Because instead of getting my heart and ass a safe distance away, say the other side of the city, once I'd tidied myself up and let him take his turn in the bathroom, I located his broom and dustpan and brush and cleaned up the hair clippings. So I was a little OCD when it came to messes. Might have been why he drove me nuts in the first place. Though his apartment was certainly neat enough now. At any rate, I couldn't leave without saying goodbye. But me departing sometime soon would definitely be for the best. Before things got even more confusing. Since my head was already dizzy with facts and feelings, it was hard to see how things could get more confusing. But, anyway.

Which was about when my cell went crazy. Texts and notifications lit up my screen. The first few were from close friends, followed by a few randoms from my past. All of them should have been in bed at this hour. Though it *was* Saturday night/Sunday morning.

"What's going on?" Adam asked, wandering out of the bedroom in a fresh pair of black jeans and a t-shirt. Freshly washed and wet hair hung down over his shoulders. The harried, haggard shadows around his eyes and face from earlier in the evening had disappeared almost completely. Sexual healing, presumably. It was irritating how easy he made looking like a walking, talking dream seem. He'd been made for gracing billboards and magazine covers, really. Also, he smelled magnificent after his shower. It was a real test of my strength not to stick my nose in his neck again. Sad but true.

I sat on the couch with my feet tucked up underneath me, trying to get a grip on the goings-on of the internet. Stunned was a good word. Followed quickly by baffled. "Someone identified me from the pictures taken downstairs."

"Shit." Any happy or calm disappeared from his face. "I'm sorry, Jill."

"I-it's okay."

He tipped his chin. "That didn't sound believable at all."

"What can I say?" I asked. "You're famous. Living in denial about it hasn't gotten me far. I guess I'll have to learn to deal with it. It's just that the songs were mostly you being a big deal from afar. These photos are...different. Oh good, they grabbed some shots off social media of me. Because I look amazing with my mouth open mid-sentence and my eyes half-closed. I told Ana not to post that photo. Ugh."

He sat down next to me, stretching his arms across the back of the couch.

I slid my finger across the screen, scrolling through the most hastily put-together nonsense article I'd ever seen in my life. "You're being painted as the hero. You valiantly came to my rescue after I had a meltdown due to our breakup. So, this is good press for you."

"Except that we broke up a year ago."

"Yeah. Wow. I sound so fragile and pathetic."

A grunt from him.

"I mean, they're not completely wrong. I was upset because of you. However, no mental breakdown is currently occurring as far as I'm aware. You're off the hook there."

His brows drew in tight. "Not sure if I should apologize again or what."

"Oh excellent, some commenters believe I'm a money-hungry ho. Little do they know, huh?"

"Fuck's sake. Don't read the comments. Rule number one in dealing with the internet: never let that crap take up room inside your skull. It leads to nowhere good."

"Oh, wait! Now they're hoping that I'll sex you and leave you again, resulting in another great album." My laughter was a brittle broken thing. "I'm so glad our emotional trauma entertains them."

Adam said a whole lot of nothing and scratched at his jawline.

"At least she's trying to put a positive spin on things, I guess." I scrolled on. "This guy says I'm a toxic bitch while he'd make you happy and treat you right. Might want to reach out for his number."

"Baby?"

"Hmm?" I looked up to find Adam wearing a pained if patient expression. "What?"

"Put the cell down."

I slowly did as I was told. That he'd called me *baby* would be ignored in totality.

"These are complete strangers casting judgement on shit they know nothing about," he said. "They don't know you or me. They don't know anything about us, okay?"

My fingers fidgeted in my lap, picking at my cuticles, a sure sign of nerves. "I've never made headlines before."

"Yeah. Well…unfortunately it's a side effect of getting to play my music." He sighed. "Since it's making news, they'll probably hang outside for a while, hoping to get another shot. Might be best if you stayed here for a bit…"

"Maybe."

"Thanks for cleaning up after the haircut." He reached out, sliding his hand over mine. I needed the contact more than I was willing to admit. Instant internet infamy was kind of nerve-wracking. His skin was so warm. The calluses on his fingers were so familiar. "I would have done it."

"Not a big deal." I shrugged, letting him hold my hand. Because I was a damn fool. "So what do you want to do? Watch TV, play guitar, do some gaming, have another nap, what?"

"Whatever you want. I'm just happy you're here."

"Adam…"

"Am I not supposed to say that?" he asked, shuffling closer. "Martha has one rule."

"Wait. Martha? Your manager?"

"That's right. If she works her ass off to give me an opportunity, then I'm not allowed to waste it."

Oh, boy. "Ha."

"This is me not wasting my chance with you."

"I wouldn't say the woman worked her ass off to get me into your car. I was willing—to a certain degree. Also, this is about you and me and doesn't involve your manager. Stop looking at me that way."

"What way?"

"Adam," I growled.

"You know, I'd kind of forgotten how good we were together."

"Had you now?"

"Figured I was just putting a shine on old memories or something," he said, moving a little closer. "Or that I was gauging the strength of the relationship off the heartache when you left, instead of really remembering what it was like when we were together. But being inside of you is sweet perfection."

"Stop it. We're not…let's not talk about the sex."

"Okay. Let's talk about you being here then. About us spending time together."

I wrinkled my nose. "Adam, you hated talking about our relationship and now that we don't even have one, you want to discuss things?"

The side of his lip curled up in a beguiling half-smile. "Sure. Why not?"

"I think my brain is about to explode."

"You know, not all of those internet comments should be ignored."

"Hmm?" I cocked my head, both bewildered and way overstimulated.

"Break my heart again, Jill." His sweet sexy smile made my heart hurt. Damn the man. "C'mon. I dare you."

Chapter Four

"That's not funny."

Adam watched me, calm as could be. "I'm not joking."

I shook my head. "I get that you're lonely, but—"

"No. Think about it," he said, tone adamant. "I'm not over you, that's the truth. Not even remotely. It's been a year, and every song is still about you. About us. Even the stuff I'm writing now. No other woman has gotten to me like you do. Tonight has made me realize I have no interest in moving on, and I think maybe deep down, you're feeling that way too."

"This may shock and stun you, but I haven't spent the last twelve months dragging my ass around being the sad girl over you." I laughed. And it was mostly true. Mostly.

"Not what I'm saying."

"Then what *are* you saying?"

He sat up straighter and stared me in the eye. "Jill, I'm better than I was. Let me show you."

"Really? Seems to me you're still hiding out in bars and making it all about the music. Which hey, it's paying off for you, and that's great. But what on earth makes you think now is the time to try and start or re-start something?" I sighed. "You're about to go to Europe, for heaven's sake. Shouldn't you be focusing on that?"

"Come with me."

Mouth hanging open and eyes wide, I couldn't have been more stunned if I tried. "W-what?"

"Come with me," he repeated. "It's a paid job. My hair needs you."

I snorted.

"You always wanted to travel. Here's your chance."

"I can't just—"

"You can. Think about it. An all-expenses-paid trip that'll help develop you professionally in a new area too." He grinned. "C'mon, this is a great idea, stop making excuses."

"Stop trying to push me," I said. "I'm not sure I want to just up and leave everything on your say-so."

"It'll all be waiting for you when you come back."

I took a deep breath. "Adam, I know you're lonely, but this is a big deal for me. I have a job and an apartment and a life here. What if you change your mind and decide that having me around isn't the constant party you seem to think it'll be?"

"You still hate your manager?"

I lifted one shoulder. "Sort of."

"They still overworking and underpaying you?"

"Y-e-a-h."

"That won't happen with me. Martha will find out what a good wage is for this sort of gig and all of your expenses will be taken care of."

My mouth hung open. He was serious. Deadly so.

"You never did like the neighborhood the apartment is in either. I'll pay out the lease, or you can with that check. Get a place you like better once we get back."

I frowned. He had a point about the neighborhood.

"Thing is, this industry is all about the ups and downs. I may not always be in a position to offer you this."

"Your fans love you."

"No, they love the latest rock star, that's all. They love *Adam Dillon*, whose songs are on everybody's lips. They love what happened to me. What I did and what I turned into. But that's not me. And it's not forever."

"I don't know."

"And this isn't about me being lonely," he tacked on.

"Are you sure about that?"

"If anything, being on tour will mean having more people around. It'll be tiring and busy as all hell, schlepping our asses all over the countryside. But it won't be lonely."

"Then what *is* it about?"

"It's about making our dreams come true. Me playing my music and you getting to travel. Both of us seeing new places and experiencing new things. This is a fucking great idea."

"And we're doing this together?"

"Yes. Together. Would that really be so bad?"

Head buzzing, I faced him. "I honestly don't know."

"We can just do it as friends if you want. Or as employer and employee. Whatever you like."

"Holy shit," I mumbled, eyes wide. "Are you actually subtly suggesting, in a roundabout manner, that you want to get back together?"

The man just shrugged. "We don't have to rush into anything. But it's not a totally bad idea. I mean, we had some good times. We worked well together for a while. Would getting back together honestly be so bad?"

"Holy shit."

"You already said that."

"Yeah, well it bears repeating." I rubbed at my temples. "My brain is overloaded. I'm surprised gory mush isn't leaking out of my ears. Before today, we hadn't even talked for almost a year. And now this."

He waved a hand in an oh-well fashion.

"I think you're thinking the sex was deep and emotional and imbued with meaning when it wasn't necessarily any of that."

"Baby, it was a quick fuck against the fridge."

"Exactly."

"I'll make up for that later if you'll let me. In the meantime, we were discussing something else that I find to be both deep and emotional."

"You've lost your mind." I massaged my throbbing temples some more. "The fame has gone to your head. You can't honestly think us getting back together is a good idea."

"Why not?"

"Where to start…"

"Jill, tell me honestly, has a single day gone by when you haven't thought of me?" He reached out, cupping my cheek in his big warm hand. "Because I know I never stopped thinking about you. That's the truth of it."

Nothing from me.

"I know you like having shit under control, but let's just roll the dice for once and see what happens. Give me a chance to make everything up to you."

For a long moment, I just stared. "Oh, boy. I don't know what to say."

"That's alright. Really." He nodded slowly, studying my face with his serious eyes. "Tell you what, let's say we sleep on it. Just sleep. No more sex. The sex seems to be freaking you out a little."

"It's a lot more than sex with you freaking me out."

"Tomorrow's Sunday so you're not working or anything, right?" he asked.

"Right."

"No big plans?"

I shook my head.

"Why don't we spend the day together and see how things go? Make a decision about all of this later when we know we're not going to immediately drive each other crazy."

"Maybe I should go home, give us both some space."

"No," he said, adamant. "Do that and we'll lose our momentum.

We're getting somewhere here, don't you think?"

I frowned.

"Plus, it's late and we're both tired. Let's just crash and see where we are in the morning. You like it here, right?" He smiled and it was so hopeful it broke my heart. "I have a new toothbrush for you and everything. That's how much of an organized adult I am these days."

"Impressive."

"Well, to be honest, Martha actually organized the buying, delivering, and possibly even the putting-away of the toothbrush. But it was totally me who thought to ask her to get it done." He grinned. "So…what do you say, Jill?"

The plan had merit, I could admit that much. And I was tired and in need of some quiet time so I could catch up with everything. So I could overthink and dissect it all. "Okay. That sounds good."

I lay on my designated side of Adam's monster of a bed—linen bedding because…fancy—staring at the faint shadows on the ceiling. Beside me, Adam's breathing was deep and even. Meanwhile, my mind was a whirl. It would not shut up. Thoughts of him and me, of Europe, of damn near everything going around and around, making for one big stressful question. What was I going to do?

I wanted to travel.

I think I even wanted to travel with Adam.

But the last time I'd invested in this man, he'd let me down big time. He broke my heart.

The man in question slept on, lying above the sheets, wearing only a pair of dark grey boxer briefs. He had such nice thighs. Very pleasant to look at. Which reminded me that when he'd been throwing all of these crazy ideas out there, we hadn't discussed if I'd be sharing his hotel room or getting my own. Would we eat meals together? How many hours a day approximately would we spend in each other's company? Was dating/living with someone on tour the same as in normal life, or did new and unexpected rules apply? Such as no girlfriends at the afterparty. Because if that was the case, he could kiss my round ass. And what about this whole signing women's boobies thing? I was so not down with that. He'd have to give up marking mammary glands or we were dead in the water right here and now.

A strong arm slung around my middle, pulling me back against the long hot length of his body. "Go to sleep, baby."

"You're not the boss of me."

"Shh." Fingers moved my hair aside, and a kiss was pressed to the back of my neck. Another very pleasant thing. "Everything will work itself out. Go to sleep."

And the bitch of it was, I did.

Following one of the best sleeps of my life, I woke up to the scent of bacon and eggs. Never a bad thing to wake up to. Unless you're a vegan, I guessed. Adam's side of the bed was empty, the sheets rumpled. Hard to tell which was the more intimate act—sleeping together or having sex. They both required a level of trust. Besides checking the time (almost eleven, yay for an awesome sleep-in!), I didn't look at my cell. Whatever had happened overnight regarding the photos of Adam and I, I didn't need to know. At least, not before coffee. The truth was, there was nothing I could do about the whole thing anyway.

"Who are you and what have you done with Adam?" I asked as I stumbled on out to the kitchen in my underwear and a borrowed tee promoting some brand of guitar strings.

He stood at the kitchen counter, scraping butter onto some toast—the kitchen counter we'd profaned last night. I tried to keep my focus on the food and the cooking, but the memories were too fresh. Whatever else this reunion had in store for us, that was at least a damn fine bit of profaning. We'd profaned the heck out of that counter.

"I was just about to come wake you. Breakfast's ready."

"You don't cook."

"I do now," he said, pushing a plate loaded with fried goodness my way. "I also pick up my dirty clothes and have even been known to do a load of laundry on occasion."

I gasped. "Good, God. How adult of you."

"I told you. I'm a whole new man. Not only can I pay my own bills, but I also get shit done, baby."

"Hmm. Are you eating?"

"I already ate."

While inspecting the food, I climbed onto a stool, getting comfortable, mindful of the mild somewhat enjoyable ache in my nether regions from our furious fucking against the fridge. Maybe having sex with him again wouldn't be the worst thing. Confusing as all hell, but still. The man would be gone to Europe soon (I wasn't awake enough to ponder the should I or shouldn't I go with him question yet). It'd probably be a good idea to get what I could while I could.

And he'd done a more than adequate job with the cooking. So the bacon edges were a bit black. They'd still taste delicious. Apparently, Adam was serious about showing me that he'd changed. Didn't mean I was any closer to taking another risk on or with him. What a crazy notion. I mean, we'd hit the wall so badly. Our breakup had been loud and angry and heart-rending. And the thought of going back there…

"Coffee," he stated, placing the steaming mug in front of me.

"Thank you. You're dressed up," I said, nodding to his pale blue button-down shirt. It was the only concession to formality, but for him, it was a notable one. His usual jeans and boots graced his lower half. His long hair had even been neatly tied back out of his gorgeous face.

"Ah, yeah." He gathered up the dirty fry pan and so on, loading up a sleek dishwasher. "Here's the thing. In all of the excitement, I forgot that Ev and Dave were throwing me a going-on-tour party today in their apartment upstairs. You'd be more than welcome, and I'd love for you to meet them. Will you come with me? Please?"

Ruh-roh. I took another sip of coffee. "More famous people?"

"More nice, down-to-earth people who'd love to meet you."

"More people who've heard those songs about me. Though everyone's heard those songs about me. But these people know you and they know...you know."

He raised his brows and took a deep breath. "Jill. Listen to me. You're overthinking this. Back in the day, Dave wrote a whole album about how Martha slept with his brother and broke his heart and then caused trouble with his new wife. It doesn't matter. They're all friends now and get along fine. They'd be the last damn people to make you feel weird about being in my songs."

"Even if the lyrics are wrong."

"I was angry at the time. We already discussed this."

"Being your muse has its downside. That's all I'm going to say about the matter," I said. "So that's what Martha was talking about? That album was about her? Wow."

The doorbell rang, and he wiped his hands on a cloth before heading over to answer it. Him making me breakfast and us hanging out in his apartment was a strangely domestic scene. I wanted to feel easy. To be relaxed. Despite the matter of me going on tour not having been raised again, it remained at the forefront of my mind. Also, we were getting along so well it was scary.

To be honest, I kept waiting for something to go wrong. For everything to go wrong.

Adam returned carrying multiple shopping bags bearing the labels of high-end boutiques. "Like I was saying, they keep things casual. But Martha thought you'd like something nice to wear. She got a local place to send some things over so you wouldn't feel the need to rush home to change or whatever. Sound good?"

"I feel like you're trying to buy my affection."

"Bullshit." He placed the bags on the counter. "If I was doing that, you'd already love me again because of the check. In all honesty, it'd be much easier. But here I am, wooing you."

"You're wooing me?" I asked with a smile.

"Me and Martha, apparently. We clearly have a Cyrano de Bergerac thing going on. What has she sent over?" He pulled out a black wool bodycon-style dress with long almost modest Chantilly lace sleeves.

I squealed in untold delight, pushing the remains of my breakfast aside. "That's new season Valentino. Give it to me."

The man did as told.

"What else is there?"

He opened a box, pushing aside numerous layers of tissue paper. "Army boots?"

"Louboutin Combat Booties. Oh, look at them, they're beautiful." I clicked my fingers. "Gimme."

"Why didn't I think of this? I should have thought of this," he mumbled. "It hasn't even occurred to you to try and shove this back in my face like you did with the check."

"They're so shiny."

"Ah…underwear, stockings, shit like that." He reported on the contents of another bag. "This one is jeans and a fluffy sweater."

"Fluffy? You mean cashmere. How lovely." I happy sighed. "It's just like Christmas but better. Your manager has amazing taste."

"Glad you approve. This one has makeup and some jewelry boxes."

"Great," I said. "You wear that battered old black leather jacket over your shirt and I'll wear the dress and boots and we'll look amazing. Trust me."

"Whatever makes you happy."

"Thought you didn't take fashion advice."

He laughed. "I don't from stylists. But I know enough to do what you tell me."

"Wise man."

"So you're good with going to the party?" he asked, a hint of a smile still lingering about his beautiful mouth.

"Oh. Absolutely."

* * * *

"Always carry sunglasses and a hat," directed *the* Lena Ferris. A fabulous curvy brunette with tortoiseshell glasses perched on her nose. She was married to the singer from Stage Dive, Jimmy Ferris. He was hanging over with the dudes on the other side of the room, drinking beers with my maybe/maybe not boyfriend. Or ex. Whatever. But the moment Adam and I had entered the apartment, the women had surrounded me. It was mildly scary but also kind of thrilling.

"Long hair is useful because if you have your head down, it kind of curtains your face, you know?" Anne demonstrated aptly, letting her red hair hide her. "Nothing to see here."

Lizzy, married to bass player Ben, sighed and ran a hand through her short, layered blond hair. "I miss being able to do that. Mind you, it only takes me a minute to wash it now, which is awesome."

"It looks fantastic," I assured her.

"Thank you."

"Just don't do what I did and hold a bag up in front of your face and then proceed to just about walk into a pole." Evelyn Ferris handed me a glass of white wine. "If Sam the bodyguard hadn't been there, I'd probably be brain dead now."

Despite the packages, Martha and her new husband Sam weren't at the party. They were apparently having alone time while they could get it what with the upcoming tour and everything. I made a mental note to thank her for the shopping next time I saw her. Assuming I saw her again.

"He keeps watching you. It's so cute." Anne peered over at Adam from behind a bottle of soda. She was off the hard stuff due to breastfeeding, her infant son currently blowing bubbles with his father. Not so surprisingly, there was dribble on both of their chins. Jimmy reached over with a rag to tend to the baby's chin. The drummer and father however was left to his own devices.

Twin girls and one boy child, all around three or four years of age, were off watching some Disney film in one of the spare bedrooms—

along with popcorn and a nanny to keep an eye on things. Ah to be rich and famous and have help with your small children. Not that I necessarily wanted kids. I didn't know about that either.

"This your first time on tour?" asked Lena.

Awkward. "Oh. Um. Yeah. I'm not sure I'm going yet."

Evelyn grinned. "But he asked you to go?"

"As tour hairdresser."

"Europe is cool," said Anne. "The summer festivals he'll be playing at are really fun."

Lena nodded. "Kind of a once-in-a-lifetime experience."

"Don't push her," chided Evelyn. "It's a big decision. And touring is hectic and exhausting, even if a bit exhilarating."

"My apologies." Lena did a half-bow from her sitting position on the couch with a flourish of the hand. "We love to see true love triumph."

"How do you know it's true love?" I asked, taking another sip of wine.

A small wicked smile curled her lips. "Because if someone wrote songs like that about me, I sure as fuck wouldn't still be sneaking hot looks at them unless they were embedded in my heart so deep, I didn't have a chance of getting them out."

"She has a point." Anne nodded.

"That damn album." I slumped back against the chair. "I mean, I'm glad he's been successful. He's super-talented. He deserves it. But I feel like it enters the room before me half the damn time, you know?"

Ev snorted. "The whole world knows the ins and outs of my relationship. Trust me, girlfriend. I hear you."

"I thought that song about Dave giving you head on the last album was just lovely," giggled Lizzy.

Ev wasted no time in lobbing a cushion at Lizzy's head. "Shut up."

"And it went to number three on the charts," said Anne.

"Should have been number one with a bullet. A small compact but highly effective travel-size bullet." Lena smacked her matte red lips together. "You kids and your sex toy euphemisms in the lyrics. So sly."

"I don't know why we're friends," said Ev with laughter in her eyes.

Lena joined in on the giggling.

"If I stay, I should just learn to suck it up. That's the lesson I'm getting here." I swirled my wine in the pretty glassware.

"Rock stars," grumbled Ev. "What the fuck can you do?"

"They're the poets of the modern generation and no topic is off-limits." Lizzy sighed. "The important thing is to not lose sight of yourself amongst all of the grime and glamor."

Willie Nelson played softly over the hidden speakers.

"Relationships can be all-encompassing. Claustrophobic even. Traveling together and working together just ups that." Anne popped a cherry tomato from the charcuterie board into her mouth. "You need to have your own life and interests and defend them vigorously."

"No, you don't!" Mal popped up behind the couch, sliding his hands down over his wife's shoulders. "I am your whole world."

"Who has the baby?" asked Anne.

"Ah, Adam. Yes. I left him with junior."

"You know Tommy freaks him out."

"Yeah. It's hilarious."

She clicked her tongue.

And sure enough, Adam was indeed frowning down at the small bundle of joy held tentatively in his arms. Adam and I as parents... What a strange idea. Tommy waved his little arms in the air while my ex watched as if the baby were about to explode or something at any moment. Not sure I'd ever seen such naked fear in his eyes. Ben the bass player sat nearby, keeping an eye on things while Dave and Jimmy both played guitars softly.

"Ben's watching him," said Mal with a smile. "Relax, pumpkin. For I am a good and noble father."

Anne smiled back at him. "I know. I just worry."

"Of course, you do." Lizzy passed her another tomato. "You two went to a lot of trouble to make him. But everything's fine, Anne.

Relax."

What I liked was the warmth these people shared. The connection they all had.

"We haven't even told you how impossible it is to be around them when they're in the middle of recording," said Ev. "It's like their minds are permanently elsewhere. All of their thinking space is taken up with creating the great work."

"That's true." Lena crossed her legs. "And that's why you need your own life and interests."

"Nonsense," said Mal, still lurking over the back of the couch. "Anne worships me, and her life couldn't be fuller."

"I work in a bookshop when I'm not on tour," reported his wife. "I love it."

"But all the books in there are about me, right?"

"Oh sure." Anne grinned. "It does imbalance the store sections a little, but I've made it work."

"Too much in the romance section, you mean?"

"Actually, it turns out most of the store is taken up with mental health books."

"Because I make you crazy in love?"

"Absolutely, that's the reason. I am crazy, and I do love you," she faithfully repeated, patting his hand. "And Tommy."

Across the room, the baby gurgled, and Adam kept right on frowning down at him. Never had I seen a grown man so perturbed by something so small. It was kind of fascinating. A little person, half me and half him. Our little person. How amazing and terrifying would that be?

"There's no rush," murmured Ev with a soft smile. "David and I have things we want to do before thinking about having children. That's still out there someday. And from what I've seen, babies are way more work than you can ever imagine."

"I believe you. But honestly, I don't even know if Adam and I should be together," I admitted, my heart on my sleeve.

She blinked. "Well, do you love him?"

God help me. "Sadly, that was never the problem."

Her smile softened even more. Like she'd been through her own share of doubts and heartache. "Take it one step at a time then, I guess. I don't know. It's easy to be smart for other people when it isn't your soul on the line. Love can hurt like a bitch. But it can be beautiful, too. David taught me that."

"Hmm."

Mal cleared his throat, leaning closer. "Thing is, even scared shitless of my small innocent child, that's the happiest I've ever seen him. Not that you can be personally responsible for someone else's happiness in life, etcetera. But if he makes you half as happy as you obviously make him, might be worth hanging around for a while. Seeing where things go."

"Huh," said Lizzy. Because this obviously wasn't an even remotely private conversation. "That was almost wise, Mal."

He sniffed as if insulted. "I'm wise. I know stuff. Tell them what I know, pumpkin."

"Stuff," she dutifully once more repeated with a smile and a wink.

"Hey. Psst. Want to run away from the party and go have sex in our apartment while our friends watch the baby?" he whispered far too loudly in her ear.

Lena snorted. "Go do it, you crazy kids. We've got Tommy."

"Yes!" Mal jumped to his feet, hands raised in the air like a boxer in his moment of victory. "Sex. Quick, pumpkin. Let's go."

There was laughter and drinks and food and music. Lots of music. Most of my friends were swinging single, living their best lives. Going to parties and having fun being free. It was interesting to be around a slightly older group who were all coupled up. Back when we were together, I'd enjoyed having a partner most of the time. Some of the time. Like Adam, he'd been my first real major important relationship. I hadn't lived with anyone else before. Not a someone I was in love with.

The more I thought about it, the more I wondered why I'd never told him I loved him. Maybe I didn't feel safe enough in the relationship. Certain enough of his attention and intentions. I didn't know.

He sat on the floor near Jimmy and David, a guitar in his lap. As Mal had said, despite being about to start his first European tour, he did indeed look relaxed and happy. And he kept looking at me. Swift glances to keep checking on me. To ensure I was okay and having fun.

"What's your next album going to be about?" asked Ben, Tommy gently being rocked to sleep in his arms.

Jimmy quirked a brow. "You've done the brokenhearted rage thing. What's next?"

Adam shot a look my way and I made sure to be busy inspecting my nails. Definitely not listening into anyone's conversation because…rude. He swallowed. "Wrote a love song this morning. Kind of more upbeat but with a blues background. Feels like that's going to set the tone for things on the new album."

"Sounds good," said Jimmy.

A nod from David Ferris. "Can only write what you're feeling."

"I wanna do something different." Adam picked out a melody on the acoustic guitar. "Going to give the other couple of rage songs I wrote to Martha to sell."

"Good money in it if you're not interested in releasing them yourself," said Ben.

My heart, meanwhile, hammered inside my chest. Adam had written a love song this morning? Something upbeat?

His head turned to the side, his gaze sliding over me. There was knowing in his eyes along with a question. I hadn't fooled him in the slightest. He knew I'd been listening and wanted to know my reaction. Apparently, mouth gaping and eyes wide was good with him. While I didn't want this to mean anything, I couldn't help but feel that it did. Adam had written me a love song. Holy shit. Just the fact turned my world upside down. With a brief satisfied smile thrown in my direction, he turned back to his friends.

Okay then. No big deal.

Deep even breaths, that was the answer. When that didn't work, I downed my half-glass of wine in one fell swoop. The man was pulling no punches. So walking away from him was going to be nigh-freaking-impossible this time around. Good to know.

With a faint smile, Ev reached over and patted my hand. "You okay?"

"He just…" Words. I had none.

"Yeah, I heard."

Nice to know I hadn't been the only one eavesdropping.

"It's big, isn't it? Looks like he's throwing it all at your feet," she said, tone low. Just between the two of us. "You just need to decide if you want it or not."

I said nothing.

"It's interesting. You have to be a certain kind of determined to make it in the music business," she continued, calm as can be. "I like seeing that focus and determination turned to other areas in their lives, you know? Can't help but feel like it means good things. A well-rounded existence or something."

"I don't know what it means. But it's freaking me the hell out."

She grabbed the bottle of white wine out of a tub of ice on the coffee table and poured me a fresh glass. "To life and love."

"I'll drink to that." Lena raised her glass.

Anne had gone to have sex and Lizzy was standing beside her husband, one hand resting on his shoulder. They were so obviously together. A unit. I didn't need that. My life would go on regardless. But I wanted that with Adam. I think I always had.

Still strumming the guitar, he glanced my way once more. I'd never had so much of his attention. Before, there'd always been other things, more important things. Now he had everything except me and I got all of the devotion I could ask for. But how long would it last?

"To life and love," I repeated and drank. What the hell?

* * * *

Adam had no sooner gotten the front door open than I was on him, tearing at his shirt, unbuttoning his jeans.

"You want something, baby?" He laughed, kicking the door closed and ripping the shirt off over his head because he was helpful like that. A couple of buttons went flying, but whatever. The boy could always buy himself more.

I had no time for words. Discussion was not required. Besides which, further talk would only complicate matters. Sex, however, could be remarkably simple. And fun.

"How drunk are you?" he asked, toeing off his boots.

"The buzz from your famous friend's expensive booze is starting to wear off, so hurry up."

He grinned. "Got it."

Goddammit. His smile was so potent. The joy in his beautiful face was sheer bliss. I couldn't *not* smile back at him, couldn't resist. But I could grab his hand and drag him into the bedroom at light speed because…priorities.

"Get naked," I ordered, half twisting to undo the zipper on the back of my fancy dress and get free of the gorgeous thing. Same went for the tiny fancy underwear and chunky ass designer combat boots. While I wanted to be buried in the outfit, right now, it all needed to be gone.

Thank goodness he had gotten the message. Boxer briefs gone, he crawled onto the big bed before collapsing into the center on his back. "Have your way with me, woman."

"Just a second."

With his gaze on my naked body, his cock was already starting to swell and harden. A sight so pretty it made my body weep with need. I crawled toward him across the mattress, a pleased smile on my face. "You kept watching me at the party."

"Just checking if you were okay."

"You wrote me a love song."

Hands behind his head, he watched. "Yes, I did."

"Are you going to play it for me?" I took him in hand, giving his dick a squeeze and a stroke, cupping the softness of his balls, just generally appreciating his goods. There was a lot to be grateful for when it came to this man.

"Whenever you want," he said, voice husky. "Just not right now."

"Hmm."

I licked my lips and took the head of his cock into my mouth, rimming the crown with a swirl of my tongue, teasing him gently with my teeth. The muscles in his thighs tensed, and his gaze darkened. When I slid him in farther, sucking long and hard, he swore harshly and low. "Fuck. Jill."

The nice thing about sucking on Adam was how wet it made me. Every little thing he did had an answering reaction in me. He groaned, and my nipples hardened. A hand grabbed hold of my hair, urging me to take him deeper, to suck him harder, and my tummy tensed, my pussy tightened. From the scent of him to the sight of him, the feel of him in my mouth and hands, it was all so good and real. Blood surged through him, making him heavier and harder. And the salty taste of pre-cum slipped onto my tongue.

"Baby," he panted. "That's enough. Up and on."

With a final kiss to his cock, I climbed up his body, positioning myself just so. He guided himself into me with one hand, the thumb of the other playing around my clit, like I wasn't swollen and wet already. Given the looks both heated and caring he'd given me all day, it was a wonder I hadn't dragged him into a bathroom at David and Ev's. Not that I thought his friends would have minded if we too had disappeared for conjugal relations.

But for some reason, I wanted him here in his bed all to myself. No need to hurry. No distractions.

The wide head of his cock pressed in as I pushed down slowly, savoring the feel of him. So thick and hard and... I gasped as he lightly pinched my nipples. I swear I blacked out for a moment. As if the fading high of the alcohol and the thrill of having him ready and willing beneath me wasn't enough. His hands on my body, ramped my need even higher, just about driving me over the edge. I'd never gotten this hot for anybody before. Not even him.

"My beautiful girl," he muttered before slapping me on the ass. "Ride me, Jill. Take what's yours, baby."

And I did as I was told. Slow to start with, rocking on him, taking my time. But that didn't last long. The friction was too good. The sight of him sweet and obscene. Sweat beaded on both our skins, and his hands grabbed my hips, urging me on. Harder, faster, more. I slammed my pelvis down on him, taking him sure and deep each time. Electricity arced up my spine, my whole body alive with sensation. And the tension just built higher and higher. The pleasure seemed insurmountable, taking me over and driving me ever onward. I never wanted it to end. But I couldn't hold it back either. The wave crashed over me, claiming me, body and soul. I was lost. Blind and broken. There were no other words for it. My body now limp and weak against his chest with his arms around me tight, it was all I could do to keep breathing.

"I think you needed that," he said, voice low. Fingers stroked my spine, tousled my hair. They never stopped moving, soothing and exciting me both. Though that might have been the feel of him still hard and ready inside me.

Though I'd dragged him into the bedroom in search of sex. No confusing emotions needed or wanted, thank you. Penis in vagina fun times here only. It didn't matter. I'd never felt so much before. Safe. Adored. Wanted. My fingertips skimmed over the firm warmth of his lips. The sharp cut of his cheekbone. The smooth soft skin of his temple. He watched me all the while. Just waiting.

"Adam…"

"Hey," he said. "Everything okay?"

I nodded. I'd lost my words again. Hell, I'd lost my mind.

Which was about when he flipped me, raising his big strong body above me, resting on his forearms. "Jill. Baby. You know I love you, right?"

I nodded, because I did know. I couldn't look at him and not know it. It would be impossible. His love was obvious now in every look. In everything he did. There could not be one iota of doubt inside me regarding Adam's love.

"Good," he said.

And then he proceeded to fuck me into oblivion.

Epilogue

The roar of the audience filled the night, the strains of an electric guitar and the deep primal beat of the drums the perfect accompaniment. I sat on an amp to the side of the stage, watching it all. Sweat dripped from Adam's long lanky frame, the smile on his face all-encompassing. Until he turned my way, that is. Then it got bigger, better, as he blew me a kiss.

"Thank you, Berlin!" He held his guitar aloft, starting on the opening of *Mine*. My new personal favorite from his next album. Not so much a love song as a having-sex-with-my-girlfriend-makes-me-very-happy kind of song. Each and every track on the album was about me and how I made him feel—in ninety-nine percent positive terms. Every couple had the occasional fight, after all.

In the three weeks we'd been on tour, things had been nonstop. Shows, promotion, and travel filled up almost every day. Occasionally, he'd get a morning or afternoon off to go sightseeing with me. Or we'd manage to slip away for a romantic dinner out somewhere. The other night, he'd wrapped a guitar string around my ring finger and tied it off before slipping it into his pocket. A measurement of my finger's circumference. Paris was in a few days. I had a really good feeling about France. A scary large level of commitment that thrilled me as well. There was no turning back now. Not for me and apparently not for him either.

He finished up the song, and the crowd roared some more. When they started stamping their feet it sounded like thunder.

"Goodnight!" Adam raised a hand, giving his guitar to a roadie and coming toward me with a grin. "Hey."

"Hey," I answered back, smacking a kiss on his sweaty face. "That was amazing."

"Eh. That was fun. *You're* amazing."

"You going to the festival afterparty?" asked Martha, appearing out of nowhere as was her way. The woman had skills. "There're a few people I wouldn't mind introducing you to."

"We've got plans," he said with no hesitation.

"Are you sure?" I asked. "I don't mind either way."

He just shook his head, slipping a hand around to the back of my neck and giving it a squeeze. Odds were, I knew exactly what our plans were, and I couldn't wait.

Martha just shrugged. Then she shot me a sly smile. "Have fun, kids."

Adam leaned in, resting his forehead against mine. "Dinner. Bath. Fucking. Lots of fucking. Maybe even some lovemaking. We'll see how we go for time."

"Sounds good."

"I love you, you know?"

I smiled. "I know. I love you too."

His big frame relaxed at the words like it had undone something within him. "Got another song in mind for the album."

"Yeah?"

"Yeah. It's a love song."

"You've written a lot of them lately."

His gaze warmed even more. "And I show no signs of stopping. It's a beautiful thing, baby."

"It is, Adam. It really is."

THE END

* * * *

Also from Kylie Scott and 1001 Dark Nights, discover Closer and Strong.

Sign up for the 1001 Dark Nights Newsletter
and be entered to win a Tiffany Key necklace.

There's a contest every month!

Go to www.1001DarkNights.com to subscribe.

**As a bonus, all subscribers can download
FIVE FREE exclusive books!**

Discover 1001 Dark Nights Collection Seven

THE BISHOP by Skye Warren
A Tanglewood Novella

TAKEN WITH YOU by Carrie Ann Ryan
A Fractured Connections Novella

DRAGON LOST by Donna Grant
A Dark Kings Novella

SEXY LOVE by Carly Phillips
A Sexy Series Novella

PROVOKE by Rachel Van Dyken
A Seaside Pictures Novella

RAFE by Sawyer Bennett
An Arizona Vengeance Novella

THE NAUGHTY PRINCESS by Claire Contreras
A Sexy Royals Novella

THE GRAVEYARD SHIFT by Darynda Jones
A Charley Davidson Novella

CHARMED by Lexi Blake
A Masters and Mercenaries Novella

SACRIFICE OF DARKNESS by Alexandra Ivy
A Guardians of Eternity Novella

THE QUEEN by Jen Armentrout
A Wicked Novella

BEGIN AGAIN by Jennifer Probst
A Stay Novella

VIXEN by Rebecca Zanetti
A Dark Protectors/Rebels Novella

SLASH by Laurelin Paige
A Slay Series Novella

THE DEAD HEAT OF SUMMER by Heather Graham
A Krewe of Hunters Novella

WILD FIRE by Kristen Ashley
A Chaos Novella

MORE THAN PROTECT YOU by Shayla Black
A More Than Words Novella

LOVE SONG by Kylie Scott
A Stage Dive Novella

CHERISH ME by J. Kenner
A Stark Ever After Novella

SHINE WITH ME by Kristen Proby
A With Me in Seattle Novella

And new from Blue Box Press:

TEASE ME by J. Kenner
A Stark International Novel

FROM BLOOD AND ASH by Jennifer L. Armentrout
A Blood and Ash Novel

QUEEN MOVE by Kennedy Ryan

THE HOUSE OF LONG AGO by Steve Berry and MJ Rose
A Cassiopeia Vitt Adventure

THE BUTTERFLY ROOM by Lucinda Riley

A KINGDOM OF FLESH AND FIRE by Jennifer L. Armentrout
A Blood and Ash Novel

Discover More Kylie Scott

Closer: A Stage Dive Novella
by Kylie Scott

When a stalker gets too close to plus-size model Mae Cooper, it's time to hire some muscle.

Enter former military man turned executive protection officer Ziggy Thayer. Having spent years guarding billionaires, royalty, and rock'n'roll greats, he's seen it all. From lavish parties through to every kind of excess.

There's no reason some Instagram stylista should throw him off his game. Even if she does have the most dangerous curves he's ever seen...

* * * *

Strong: A Stage Dive Novella
by Kylie Scott

When the girl of your dreams is kind of a nightmare.

As head of security to Stage Dive, one of the biggest rock bands in the world, Sam Knowles has plenty of experience dealing with trouble. But spoilt brat Martha Nicholson just might be the worst thing he's ever encountered. The beautiful troublemaker claims to have reformed, but Sam knows better than to think with what's in his pants. Unfortunately, it's not so easy to make his heart fall into line.

Martha's had her sights on the seriously built bodyguard for years. Quiet and conservative, he's not even remotely her type. So why the hell can't she get him out of her mind? There's more to her than the Louboutin wearing party-girl of previous years, however. Maybe it's time to let him in on that fact and deal with this thing between them.

About Kylie Scott

Kylie is a New York Times and USA Today best-selling author. She was voted Australian Romance Writer of the year, 2013, 2014, & 2018 by the Australian Romance Writers' Association and her books have been translated into eleven different languages.

Discover 1001 Dark Nights

COLLECTION ONE
FOREVER WICKED by Shayla Black
CRIMSON TWILIGHT by Heather Graham
CAPTURED IN SURRENDER by Liliana Hart
SILENT BITE: A SCANGUARDS WEDDING by Tina Folsom
DUNGEON GAMES by Lexi Blake
AZAGOTH by Larissa Ione
NEED YOU NOW by Lisa Renee Jones
SHOW ME, BABY by Cherise Sinclair
ROPED IN by Lorelei James
TEMPTED BY MIDNIGHT by Lara Adrian
THE FLAME by Christopher Rice
CARESS OF DARKNESS by Julie Kenner

COLLECTION TWO
WICKED WOLF by Carrie Ann Ryan
WHEN IRISH EYES ARE HAUNTING by Heather Graham
EASY WITH YOU by Kristen Proby
MASTER OF FREEDOM by Cherise Sinclair
CARESS OF PLEASURE by Julie Kenner
ADORED by Lexi Blake
HADES by Larissa Ione
RAVAGED by Elisabeth Naughton
DREAM OF YOU by Jennifer L. Armentrout
STRIPPED DOWN by Lorelei James
RAGE/KILLIAN by Alexandra Ivy/Laura Wright
DRAGON KING by Donna Grant
PURE WICKED by Shayla Black
HARD AS STEEL by Laura Kaye
STROKE OF MIDNIGHT by Lara Adrian
ALL HALLOWS EVE by Heather Graham
KISS THE FLAME by Christopher Rice
DARING HER LOVE by Melissa Foster
TEASED by Rebecca Zanetti
THE PROMISE OF SURRENDER by Liliana Hart

COLLECTION THREE
HIDDEN INK by Carrie Ann Ryan
BLOOD ON THE BAYOU by Heather Graham
SEARCHING FOR MINE by Jennifer Probst
DANCE OF DESIRE by Christopher Rice
ROUGH RHYTHM by Tessa Bailey
DEVOTED by Lexi Blake
Z by Larissa Ione
FALLING UNDER YOU by Laurelin Paige
EASY FOR KEEPS by Kristen Proby
UNCHAINED by Elisabeth Naughton
HARD TO SERVE by Laura Kaye
DRAGON FEVER by Donna Grant
KAYDEN/SIMON by Alexandra Ivy/Laura Wright
STRUNG UP by Lorelei James
MIDNIGHT UNTAMED by Lara Adrian
TRICKED by Rebecca Zanetti
DIRTY WICKED by Shayla Black
THE ONLY ONE by Lauren Blakely
SWEET SURRENDER by Liliana Hart

COLLECTION FOUR
ROCK CHICK REAWAKENING by Kristen Ashley
ADORING INK by Carrie Ann Ryan
SWEET RIVALRY by K. Bromberg
SHADE'S LADY by Joanna Wylde
RAZR by Larissa Ione
ARRANGED by Lexi Blake
TANGLED by Rebecca Zanetti
HOLD ME by J. Kenner
SOMEHOW, SOME WAY by Jennifer Probst
TOO CLOSE TO CALL by Tessa Bailey
HUNTED by Elisabeth Naughton
EYES ON YOU by Laura Kaye
BLADE by Alexandra Ivy/Laura Wright
DRAGON BURN by Donna Grant

TRIPPED OUT by Lorelei James
STUD FINDER by Lauren Blakely
MIDNIGHT UNLEASHED by Lara Adrian
HALLOW BE THE HAUNT by Heather Graham
DIRTY FILTHY FIX by Laurelin Paige
THE BED MATE by Kendall Ryan
NIGHT GAMES by CD Reiss
NO RESERVATIONS by Kristen Proby
DAWN OF SURRENDER by Liliana Hart

COLLECTION FIVE
BLAZE ERUPTING by Rebecca Zanetti
ROUGH RIDE by Kristen Ashley
HAWKYN by Larissa Ione
RIDE DIRTY by Laura Kaye
ROME'S CHANCE by Joanna Wylde
THE MARRIAGE ARRANGEMENT by Jennifer Probst
SURRENDER by Elisabeth Naughton
INKED NIGHTS by Carrie Ann Ryan
ENVY by Rachel Van Dyken
PROTECTED by Lexi Blake
THE PRINCE by Jennifer L. Armentrout
PLEASE ME by J. Kenner
WOUND TIGHT by Lorelei James
STRONG by Kylie Scott
DRAGON NIGHT by Donna Grant
TEMPTING BROOKE by Kristen Proby
HAUNTED BE THE HOLIDAYS by Heather Graham
CONTROL by K. Bromberg
HUNKY HEARTBREAKER by Kendall Ryan
THE DARKEST CAPTIVE by Gena Showalter

COLLECTION SIX
DRAGON CLAIMED by Donna Grant
ASHES TO INK by Carrie Ann Ryan
ENSNARED by Elisabeth Naughton
EVERMORE by Corinne Michaels

VENGEANCE by Rebecca Zanetti
ELI'S TRIUMPH by Joanna Wylde
CIPHER by Larissa Ione
RESCUING MACIE by Susan Stoker
ENCHANTED by Lexi Blake
TAKE THE BRIDE by Carly Phillips
INDULGE ME by J. Kenner
THE KING by Jennifer L. Armentrout
QUIET MAN by Kristen Ashley
ABANDON by Rachel Van Dyken
THE OPEN DOOR by Laurelin Paige
CLOSER by Kylie Scott
SOMETHING JUST LIKE THIS by Jennifer Probst
BLOOD NIGHT by Heather Graham
TWIST OF FATE by Jill Shalvis
MORE THAN PLEASURE YOU by Shayla Black
WONDER WITH ME by Kristen Proby
THE DARKEST ASSASSIN by Gena Showalter

Discover Blue Box Press

TAME ME by J. Kenner
TEMPT ME by J. Kenner
DAMIEN by J. Kenner
TEASE ME by J. Kenner
REAPER by Larissa Ione
THE SURRENDER GATE by Christopher Rice
SERVICING THE TARGET by Cherise Sinclair

On behalf of 1001 Dark Nights,

Liz Berry, M.J. Rose, and Jillian Stein would like to thank ~

Steve Berry
Doug Scofield
Benjamin Stein
Kim Guidroz
Social Butterfly PR
Ashley Wells
Asha Hossain
Chris Graham
Chelle Olson
Kasi Alexander
Jessica Johns
Dylan Stockton
Richard Blake
and Simon Lipskar

Made in the USA
Columbia, SC
18 October 2020